TWENTY-FOUR HOURS
IN THE LIFE OF
A WOMAN

THE ROYAL GAME

STEFAN ZWEIG was born in 1881 in Vienna, a member of a wealthy Austrian-Jewish family. He studied in Berlin and Vienna and was first known as a poet and translator, then as a librettist and biographer. His stories and novellas were collected in 1934. Zweig travelled widely, living in Salzburg between the wars, and enjoying literary fame. In 1934, with the rise of Nazism, he briefly moved to London, taking British citizenship. After a short period in New York, he settled in Brazil where, in 1942, he and his wife were found dead in bed, in an apparent double suicide.

STEFAN ZWEIG

TWENTY-FOUR HOURS IN THE LIFE OF A WOMAN

THE ROYAL GAME

PUSHKIN PRESS
LONDON

Every Night & every Morn
Some to Misery are Born.
Every Morn & every Night
Some are Born to sweet delight.
Some are Born to sweet delight,
Some are Born to Endless Night.

From AUGURIES OF INNOCENCE
William Blake

Original texts © Williams Verlag A.G. Zurich

Twenty-four Hours in the Life of a Woman
First published in German as
Vierundzwanzig Stunden im Leben einer Frau in 1927
First published by Pushkin Press in 2003

English translation © Anthea Bell

The Royal Game
First published in German as
Schachnovelle in 1941
First published in this translation in 1944
First published by Pushkin Press in 2001

English translation © B W Huebsch

This edition published in 2006 by
Pushkin Press
12 Chester Terrace
London N1 4ND

British Library Cataloguing in Publication Data:
A catalogue record for this book is available
from the British Library

ISBN (13) 978 1 901285 61 1
ISBN (10) 1 901285 61 8

Cover: *Baccarat—The Fur Cape* 1920
© Estate of Walter R Sickert
& Tate London 2005
All Rights Reserved DACS

Frontispiece: Portrait of Stefan Zweig
© Roger-Viollet Rex Features

Set in 10.5 on 13.5 Baskerville
and printed in Jordan by National Press

TWENTY-FOUR HOURS
IN THE LIFE OF
A WOMAN

Translated from the German by Anthea Bell

IN THE LITTLE GUEST-HOUSE on the Riviera where I was staying at the time, ten years before the war, a heated discussion had broken out at our table and unexpectedly threatened to degenerate into frenzied argument, even rancour and recrimination. Most people have little imagination. If something doesn't affect them directly, does not drive a sharp wedge straight into their minds, it hardly excites them at all; but if an incident, however slight, takes place before their eyes, close enough for the senses to perceive it, it instantly rouses them to extremes of passion. They compensate for the infrequency of their sympathy, as it were, by exhibiting disproportionate and excessive vehemence.

Such was the case that day among our thoroughly bourgeois company at table, where on the whole we just made equable small talk and cracked mild little jokes, usually parting as soon as the meal was over: the German husband and wife to go on excursions and take snapshots, the portly Dane to set out on tedious fishing expeditions, the distinguished English lady to return to her books, the Italian married couple to indulge in escapades to Monte Carlo, and I to lounge in a garden chair or get some work done. This time, however, our irate discussion left us all still very much at odds, and if someone suddenly rose it was not, as usual, to take civil leave of the rest of us, but in a mood of heated irascibility that, as I have said, was assuming positively frenzied form.

The incident obsessing our little party, admittedly, was odd enough. From outside, the guest-house where the seven of us were staying might have been an isolated villa—with a wonderful view of the rock-strewn beach from its windows—but in fact it was only the cheaper annexe of the Grand Palace Hotel to which it was directly linked by the garden, so that we in the guest-house were in constant touch with the hotel guests. And that same hotel had been the scene of an outright scandal the day before, when a young Frenchman had arrived by the midday train, at twenty past twelve (I can't avoid giving the time so precisely because it was of importance to the incident itself, and indeed to the subject of our agitated conversation), and took a room with a view of the sea, opening straight on to the beach, which in itself indicated that he was in reasonably easy circumstances. Not only his discreet elegance but, most of all, his extraordinary and very appealing good looks made an attractive impression. A silky blond moustache surrounded sensuously warm lips in a slender, girlish face; soft, wavy brown hair curled over his pale forehead; every glance of his melting eyes was a caress—indeed everything about him was soft, endearing, charming, but without any artifice or affectation. At a distance he might at first remind you slightly of those pink wax dummies to be seen adopting dandified poses in the window displays of large fashion stores, walking-stick in hand and representing the ideal of male beauty, but closer inspection dispelled any impression of foppishness, for—most unusually— his charm was natural and innate, and seemed an inseparable part of him. He greeted everyone individually in passing, in a manner as warm as it was modest, and it was a pleasure to see his unfailingly graceful demeanour unaffectedly brought into play on every occasion. When a lady was going to the cloakroom he made haste to fetch her coat, he had a friendly glance or joke for every child, he was both affable and discreet—in short, he seemed to be one of those happy souls who, secure in the knowledge that their bright faces and youthful attractions are pleasing to others, transmute that security anew into yet more charm. His presence worked wonders among the hotel guests, most of whom were elderly and sickly, and he irresistibly won everyone's liking with the victorious bearing of youth, that flush of ease and liveliness with which charm so delightfully endows some human beings. Only a couple of hours after his arrival he was playing tennis with the two daughters of the stout, thick-set manufacturer from Lyon, twelve-year-old Annette and thirteen-year-old Blanche, and their mother, the refined, delicate and reserved Madame Henriette, smiled slightly to see her inexperienced daughters unconsciously flirting with the young stranger. That evening he watched for an hour as we played chess, telling a few amusing anecdotes now and then in an unobtrusive style, strolled along the terrace again with Madame Henriette while her husband played dominoes with a business friend as usual; and late in the evening I saw him in suspiciously intimate conversation with the hotel secretary in the dim light of her office. Next morning he went fishing with my Danish chess partner, showing a remarkable knowledge of angling, and then held a long conversation about politics with the Lyon manufacturer in which he also proved himself an entertaining companion, for the stout Frenchman's hearty laughter could be heard above the sound of the breaking waves. After lunch he spent an hour alone with Madame Henriette in the garden again, drinking black coffee, played another game of tennis with her daughters, and chatted in the lobby to the German couple. At six o'clock I met him at the railway station when I went to post a letter. He strode quickly towards me and said, as if apologetically, that he had been suddenly called away but would be back in two days' time. Sure enough, he was absent from the dining-room that evening, but only in person, for he was the sole subject of conversation at every table, and all the guests praised his delightful, cheerful nature.

That night, I suppose at about eleven o'clock, I was sitting in my room finishing a book when I suddenly heard agitated shouts and cries from the garden coming in through my open window. Something was obviously going on over at the hotel. Feeling concerned rather than curious, I immediately hurried

13

across—it was some fifty paces—and found the guests and staff milling around in great excitement. Madame Henriette, whose husband had been playing dominoes with his friend from Namur as usual, had not come back from her evening walk on the terrace by the beach, and it was feared that she had suffered an accident. The normally ponderous, slow-moving manufacturer kept charging down to the beach like a bull, and when he called: "Henriette! Henriette!" into the night, his voice breaking with fear, the sound conveyed something of the terror and the primaeval nature of a gigantic animal wounded to death. The waiters and pageboys ran up and down the stairs in agitation, all the guests were woken and the police were called. The fat man, however, trampled and stumbled his way through all this, waistcoat unbuttoned, sobbing and shrieking as he pointlessly shouted the name "Henriette! Henriette!" into the darkness. By now the children were awake upstairs, and stood at the window in their night-dresses, calling down for their mother. Their father hurried upstairs again to comfort them.

And then something so terrible happened that it almost defies retelling, for a violent strain on human nature, at moments of extremity, can often give such tragic expression to a man's bearing that no images or words can reproduce it with the same lightning force. Suddenly the big, heavy man came down the creaking stairs with a changed look on his face, very weary and yet grim. He had a letter in his hand. "Call them all back!" he told the hotel major-domo, in a barely audible voice. "Call everyone in again. There's no need. My wife has left me."

Mortally wounded as he was, the man showed composure, a tense, superhuman composure as he faced all the people standing around, looking at him curiously as they pressed close and then suddenly turned away again, each of them feeling alarmed, ashamed and confused. He had just enough strength left to make his way unsteadily past us, looking at no one, and switch off the light in the reading-room. We heard the sound of his ponderous, massive body dropping heavily into an arm-chair, and then a wild, animal sobbing, the weeping of a man who has never wept before. That elemental pain had a kind of paralysing power over every one of us, even the least of those present. None of the waiters, none of the guests who had joined the throng out of curiosity, ventured either a smile or a word of condolence. Silently, one by one, as if put to shame by so shattering an emotional outburst, we crept back to our rooms, while that stricken specimen of mankind shook and sobbed alone with himself in the dark as the building slowly laid itself to rest, whispering, muttering, murmuring and sighing.

You will understand that such an event, striking like light-ning before our very eyes and our perceptions, was likely to cause considerable turmoil in persons usually accustomed to an easy-going existence and carefree pastimes. But while this extraordinary incident was certainly the point of departure for the discussion that broke out so vehemently at our table, almost bringing us to blows, in essence the dispute was more fundamental, an angry conflict between two warring concepts of life. For it soon became known from the indiscretion of a chambermaid who had read the letter—in his helpless fury, the devastated husband had crumpled it up and dropped it on the floor somewhere—that Madame Henriette had not left alone but, by mutual agreement, with the young Frenchman (for whom most people's liking now swiftly began to evaporate). At first glance, of course, it might seem perfectly understand-able for this minor Madame Bovary to exchange her stout, provincial husband for an elegant and handsome young fellow. But what aroused so much indignation in all present was the circumstance that neither the manufacturer nor his daughters, nor even Madame Henriette herself, had ever set eyes on this Lovelace before, and consequently their evening conversation for a couple of hours on the terrace, and the one-hour session in the garden over black coffee, seemed to have sufficed to make a woman about thirty-three years old and of blameless reputation abandon her husband and two children overnight, following a young dandy previously unknown to her without a second thought. This apparently evident fact was unanimously condemned at our table as perfidious deceit and a cunning manoeuvre on the part of the two lovers: of course Madame Henriette must have been conducting a clandestine affair with the young man long before, and he had come here, Pied Piper that he was, only to settle the final details of their flight, for—so our company deduced—it was out of the question for a decent woman who had known a man a mere couple of hours to run off just like that when he first whistled her up. It amused me to take a different view, and I energetically defended such an eventuality as possible, even probable in a woman who at heart had perhaps been ready to take some decisive action through all the years of a tedious, disappointing marriage. My unexpected opposition quickly made the discussion more general, and it became particularly agitated when both married couples, the Germans and the Italians alike, denied the existence of the *coup de foudre* with positively scornful indignation, condemning it as folly and tasteless romantic fantasy.

Well, it's of no importance here to go back in every detail over the stormy course of an argument conducted between soup and dessert: only professionals of the *table d'hôte* are witty, and points made in the heat of a chance dispute at table are usually banal, since the speakers resort to them clumsily and in haste. It is also difficult to explain how our discussion came to assume the form of insulting remarks so quickly; I think it grew so vehement in the first place because of the instinctive wish of both husbands to reassure themselves that their own wives were incapable of such shallow inconstancy. Unfortunately they could find no better way of expressing their feelings than to tell me that no one could speak as I did except a man who judged the feminine psyche by a bachelor's random conquests, which came only too cheap. This accusation rather annoyed me, and when the German lady added her mite by remarking instructively that there were real women on the one hand and 'natural-born tarts' on the other, and in her opinion Madame Henriette must have been one of the latter, I lost patience entirely and became aggressive myself. Such a denial of the obvious fact that at certain times in her life a woman is delivered up to mysterious powers beyond her own will and judgement, I said, merely concealed fear of our own instincts, of the demonic element in our nature, and many people seemed to take pleasure in feeling themselves stronger, purer and more moral that those who are 'easily led astray'. Personally, I added, I thought it more honourable for a woman to follow her instincts freely and passionately than to betray her husband in his own arms with her eyes closed, as so many did. Such, roughly, was the gist of my remarks, and the more the others attacked poor Madame Henriette in a conversation now rising to fever pitch, the more passionately I defended her (going far beyond what I actually felt in the case). My enthusiasm amounted to what in student circles might have been described as a challenge to the two married couples, and as a not very harmonious quartet they went for me with such indignant solidarity that the old Dane, who was sitting there with a jovial expression, much like the referee at a football match with stopwatch in hand, had to tap his knuckles on the table from time to time in admonishment. "Gentlemen, please!" But it never worked for long. One of the husbands had jumped up from the table three times already, red in the face, and could be calmed by his wife only with difficulty—in short, a dozen minutes more and our discussion would have ended in violence, had not Mrs C suddenly poured oil on the stormy waters of the conversation.

Mrs C, the white-haired, distinguished old English lady, presided over our table as unofficial arbiter. Sitting very up-right in her place, turning to everyone with the same uniform friendliness, saying little and yet listening with the most gratifying interest, she was a pleasing sight from the purely physical viewpoint, and an air of wonderfully calm composure emanated from her aristocratically reserved nature. Up to a certain point she kept her distance from the rest of us, although she could also show special kindness with tactful delicacy: she spent most of her time in the garden reading books, and sometimes played the piano, but she was seldom to be seen in company or deep in conversation. You scarcely noticed her, yet she exerted a curious influence over us all, for no sooner did she now, for the first time, intervene in our discussion than we all felt, with embarrassment, that we had been too loud and intemperate.

Mrs C had made use of the awkward pause when the German gentleman jumped brusquely up and was then induced to sit quietly down again. Unexpectedly, she raised her clear, grey eyes, looked at me indecisively for a moment, and then, with almost objective clarity, took up the subject in her own way.

"So you think, if I understand you correctly, that Madame Henriette—that a woman can be cast unwittingly into a sudden adventure, can do things that she herself would have thought impossible an hour earlier, and for which she can hardly be held responsible?"

"I feel sure of it, ma'am."

"But then all moral judgements would be meaningless, and any kind of vicious excess could be justified. If you really think that a *crime passionnel*, as the French call it, is no crime at all, then what is the state judiciary for? It doesn't take a great deal of good will—and you yourself have a remarkable amount of that" she added, with a slight smile, "to see passion in every crime, and use that passion to excuse it."

The clear yet almost humorous tone of her words did me good, and instinctively adopting her objective stance I answered half in jest, half in earnest myself: "I'm sure that the state judiciary takes a more severe view of such things than I do; its duty is to protect morality and convention without regard for pity, so it is obliged to judge and make no excuses. But as a private person I don't see why I should voluntarily assume the role of public prosecutor. I'd prefer to appear for the defence. Personally, I'd rather understand others than condemn them."

Mrs C looked straight at me for a while with her clear grey eyes, and hesitated. I began to fear she had failed to understand what I said, and was preparing to repeat it in English. But with a curious gravity, as if conducting an examination, she continued with her questions.

"Don't you think it contemptible or shocking, though, for a woman to leave her husband and her children to follow some chance-met man, when she can't even know if he is worth her love? Can you really excuse such reckless, promiscuous conduct in a woman who is no longer in her first youth, and should have disciplined herself to preserve her self-respect, if only for the sake of her children?"

"I repeat, ma'am," I persisted, "that I decline to judge or condemn her in this case. To you, I can readily admit that I was exaggerating a little just now—poor Madame Henriette is certainly no heroine, not even an adventuress by nature, let alone a *grande amoureuse*. So far as I know her, she seems to me just an average, fallible woman. I do feel a little respect for her because she bravely followed the dictates of her own will, but even more pity, since tomorrow, if not today, she is sure to be deeply unhappy. She may have acted unwisely and certainly too hastily, but her conduct was not base or mean, and I still challenge anyone's right to despise the poor unfortunate woman."

"And what about you yourself; do you still feel exactly the same respect and esteem for her? Don't you see any difference between the woman you knew the day before yesterday as a respectable wife, and the woman who ran off with a perfect stranger a day later?"

"None at all. Not the slightest, not the least difference."

"*Is that so?*" She instinctively spoke those words in English; the whole conversation seemed to be occupying her mind to a remarkable degree. After a brief moment's thought, she raised her clear eyes to me again, with a question in them.

"And suppose you were to meet Madame Henriette tomorrow, let's say in Nice on the young man's arm, would you still greet her?"

"Of course."

"And speak to her?"

"Of course."

"If—if you were married, would you introduce such a woman to your wife as if nothing had happened?"

"Of course."

"*Would you really?*" she said, in English again, speaking in tones of incredulous astonishment.

"*Indeed I would,*" I answered, unconsciously falling into English too.

Mrs C was silent. She still seemed to be thinking hard, and suddenly, looking at me as if amazed at her own courage, she said: "I don't know if I would. Perhaps I might." And with the indefinable and peculiarly English ability to end a conversation firmly but without brusque discourtesy, she rose and offered me her hand in a friendly gesture. Her intervention had restored peace, and we were all privately grateful to her for ensuring that although we had been at daggers drawn a moment ago, we could speak to each other with tolerable civility again. The dangerously charged atmosphere was relieved by a few light remarks.

Although our discussion seemed to have been courteously resolved, its irate bitterness had none the less left a faint, lingering sense of estrangement between me and my opponents in argument. The German couple behaved with reserve, while over the next few days the two Italians enjoyed asking me ironically, at frequent intervals, whether I had heard anything of '*la cara signora Henrietta.*' Urbane as our manners might appear, something of the equable, friendly good fellowship of our table had been irrevocably destroyed.

The chilly sarcasm of my adversaries was made all the more obvious by the particular friendliness Mrs C had shown me since our discussion. Although she was usually very reserved, and hardly ever seemed to invite conversation with her table companions outside meal times, she now on several occasions found an opportunity to speak to me in the garden and—I might almost say—distinguish me by her attention, for her upper-class reserve made a private talk with her seem a special favour. To be honest, in fact, I must say she positively sought me out and took every opportunity of entering into conversation with me, in so marked a way that had she not been a white-haired elderly lady I might have entertained some strange, conceited ideas. But when we talked our conversation inevitably and without fail came back to the same point of departure, to Madame Henriette: it seemed to give her some mysterious pleasure to accuse the errant wife of weakness of character and irresponsibility. At the same time, however, she seemed to enjoy my steadfast defence of that refined and delicate woman, and my insistence that nothing could ever make me deny my sympathy for her. She constantly steered our conversation the same way, and in the end I hardly knew what to make of her strange, almost eccentric obsession with the subject.

This went on for a few days, maybe five or six, and she never said a word to suggest why this kind of conversation had assumed importance for her. But I could not help realising that it had when I happened to mention, during a walk, that my stay here would soon be over, and I thought of leaving the day after tomorrow. At this her usually serene face suddenly assumed a curiously intense expression, and something like the shadow of a cloud came into her clear grey eyes. "Oh, what a pity! There's still so much I'd have liked to discuss with you." And from then on a certain uneasy restlessness showed that while she spoke she was thinking of something else, something that occupied and distracted her mind a great deal. At last she herself seemed disturbed by this mental distraction, for in the middle of a silence that had suddenly fallen between us she unexpectedly offered me her hand.

"I see that I can't put what I really want to say to you clearly. I'd rather write it down." And walking faster than I was used to seeing her move, she went towards the house.

I did indeed find a letter in her energetic, frank handwriting in my room just before dinner that evening. I now greatly regret my carelessness with written documents in my youth, which means that I cannot reproduce her note word for word, and can give only the gist of her request: might she, she asked, tell me about an episode in her life? It lay so far back in the past, she wrote, that it was hardly a part of her present existence any more, and the fact that I was leaving the day after tomorrow made it easier for her to speak of something that had occupied and preyed on her mind for over twenty years. If I did not feel such a conversation was an importunity, she would like to ask me for an hour of my time.

The letter—I merely outline its contents here—fascinated me to an extraordinary degree: its English style alone lent it great clarity and resolution. Yet I did not find it easy to answer. I tore up three drafts before I replied:

'I am honoured by your showing such confidence in me, and I promise you an honest response should you require one. Of course I cannot ask you to tell me more than your heart dictates. But whatever you tell, tell yourself and me the truth. Please believe me: I feel your confidence a special honour.'

The note made its way to her room that evening, and I received the answer next morning:

'You are quite right: half the truth is useless, only the whole truth is worth telling. I shall do my best to hide nothing from myself or from you. Please come to my room after dinner—at the age of sixty-seven, I need fear no misinterpretation, but I cannot speak freely in the garden, or with other people near by. Believe me, I did not find it easy to make my mind up to take this step.'

During the day we met again at table and discussed indifferent matters in the conventional way. But when we encountered each other in the garden she avoided me in obvious confusion, and I felt it both painful and moving to see this white-haired old lady fleeing from me down an avenue lined with pine trees, as shy as a young girl.

At the appointed time that evening I knocked on her door, and it was immediately opened; the room was bathed in soft twilight, with only the little reading lamp on the table casting a circle of yellow light in the dusk. Mrs C came towards me without any self-consciousness, offered me an armchair and sat down opposite me. I sensed that she had prepared mentally for each of these movements, but then came a pause, obviously unplanned, a pause that grew longer and longer as she came to a difficult decision. I dared not inject any remark into this pause, for I sensed a strong will wrestling with great resistance here. Sometimes the faint notes of a waltz drifted up from the drawing-room below, and I listened intently, as if to relieve the silence of some of its oppressive quality. She too seemed to feel the unnatural tension of the silence awkward, for she suddenly pulled herself together to take the plunge, and began.

"It's only the first few words that are so difficult. For the last two days I have been preparing to be perfectly clear and truthful; I hope I shall succeed. Perhaps you don't yet understand why I am telling all this to you, a stranger, but not a day, scarcely an hour goes by when I do not think of this particular incident, and you can believe me, an old woman now, when I say it is intolerable to spend one's whole life staring at a single point in it, a single day. Everything I am about to tell you, you see, happened within the space of just twenty-four hours in my sixty-seven years of life, and I have often asked myself, I have wondered to the point of madness, why a moment's foolish action on a single occasion should matter. But we cannot shake off what we so vaguely call conscience, and when I heard you speak so objectively of Madame Henriette's case I thought that perhaps there might be an end to my senseless dwelling on the past, my constant self-accusation, if I could bring myself to speak freely to someone, anyone, about that single day in my life. If I were not an Anglican but a Catholic, the confessional would long ago have offered me an opportunity of release by putting what I have kept silent into words—but that comfort is denied us, and so I make this strange attempt to absolve myself by speaking to you today. I know all this sounds very odd, but you agreed unhesitatingly to my suggestion, and I am grateful.

As I said, I would like to tell you about just one day in my life—all the rest of it seems to me insignificant and would be tedious listening for anyone else. There was nothing in the least out of the ordinary in the course of it until my forty-second year. My parents were rich landlords in Scotland, we owned large factories and leased out land, and in the usual way of the gentry in my country we spent most of the year on our estates but went to London for the season. I met my future husband at a party when I was eighteen. He was a second son of the well-known R family, and had served with the army in India for ten years. We soon married, and led the carefree life of our social circle: three months of the year in London, three months on our estates, and the rest of the time in hotels in Italy, Spain and France. Not the slightest shadow ever clouded our marriage, and we had two sons who are now grown up. When I was forty my husband suddenly died. He had returned from his years in the tropics with a liver complaint, and I lost him within the space of two terrible weeks. My elder son was already in the army, my younger son at university—so I was left entirely alone overnight, and used as I was to affectionate companionship, that loneliness was a torment to me. I felt I could not stay a day longer in the desolate house where every object reminded me of the tragic loss of my beloved husband, and so I decided that while my sons were still unmarried, I would spend much of the next few years travelling.

In essence, I regarded my life from that moment on as entirely pointless and useless. The man with whom I had shared every hour and every thought for twenty-three years was dead, my children did not need me, I was afraid of casting a cloud over their youth with my sadness and melancholy—but I wished and desired nothing any more for myself. I went first to Paris, where I visited shops and museums out of sheer boredom, but the city and everything else were strange to me, and I avoided company because I could not bear the polite sympathy in other people's eyes when they saw that I was in mourning. How those months of aimless, apathetic wandering passed I can hardly say now; all I know is that I had a constant wish to die, but not the strength to hasten the end I longed for so ardently.

In my second year of mourning, that is to say my forty-second year, I had come to Monte Carlo at the end of March in my unacknowledged flight from time that had become worthless and was more than I could deal with. To be honest, I came there out of tedium, out of the painful emptiness of the heart that wells up like nausea, and at least tries to nourish itself on small external stimulations. The less I felt in myself, the more strongly I was drawn to those places where the whirligig of life spins most rapidly. If you are experiencing nothing yourself, the passionate restlessness of others stimulates the nervous system like music or drama.

That was why I quite often went to the casino. I was intrigued to see the tide of delight or dismay ebbing and flowing in other people's faces, while my own heart lay at such a low ebb. In addition my husband, although never frivolous, had enjoyed visiting such places now and then, and with a certain unintentional piety I remained faithful to his old habits. And there in the casino began those twenty-four hours that were more thrilling than any game, and disturbed my life for years.

I had dined at midday with the Duchess of M, a relation of my family, and after supper I didn't feel tired enough to go to bed yet. So I went to the gaming hall, strolled among the tables without playing myself, and watched the mingled company in my own special way. I repeat, in my own special way, the way my dead husband had once taught me when, tired of watching, I complained of the tedium of looking at the same faces all the time: the wizened old women who sat for hours before venturing a single jetton, the cunning professionals, the *demi-mondaines* of the card table, all that dubious chance-met company which, as you'll know, is considerably less picturesque and romantic than it is always painted in silly novels, where you might think it the *fleur d'élégance* and aristocracy of Europe. Yet the casino of twenty years ago, when real money, visible and tangible, was staked and crackling banknotes, gold Napoleons and pert little five-franc pieces rained down, was far more attractive than it is today, with a solid set of folk on Cook's Tours tediously frittering their characterless gaming chips away in the grand, fashionably renovated citadel of gambling. Even then, however, I found little to stimulate me in the similarity of so many indifferent faces, until one day my husband, whose private passion was for chiromancy—that's to say, divination by means of the hand—showed me an unusual method of observation which proved much more interesting, exciting and fascinating than standing casually around. In this method you never look at a face, only at the rectangle of the table, and on the table only at the hands of the players and the way they move. I don't know if you yourself ever happen to have looked at the green table, just that green square with the ball in the middle of it tumbling drunkenly from number to number, while fluttering scraps of paper, round silver and gold coins fall like seed-corn on the spaces of the board, to be raked briskly away by the croupier or shovelled over to the winner like harvest bounty. If you watch from that angle, only the hands change—all those pale, moving, waiting hands around the green table, all emerging from the ever-different caverns of the players' sleeves, each a beast of prey ready to leap, each varying in shape and colour, some bare, others laden with rings and clinking bracelets, some hairy like wild beasts, some damp and writhing like eels, but all of them tense, vibrating with a vast impatience. I could never help thinking of a racecourse where the excited horses are held back with difficulty on the starting line in case they gallop away too soon; they quiver and buck and rear in just the same way. You can tell everything from those hands, from the way they wait, they grab, they falter; you can see an avaricious character in a claw-like hand and a spendthrift in a relaxed one, a calculating man in a steady hand and a desperate man in a trembling wrist; hundreds of characters betray themselves instantly in their way of handling money, crumpling or nervously creasing notes, or letting it lie as the ball goes round, their hands now weary and exhausted. Human beings give themselves away in play—a cliché, I know, but I would say their own hands give them away even more clearly in gambling. Almost all gamblers soon learn to control their faces—from the neck up, they wear the cold mask of impassivity; they force away the lines around their mouths and hide their agitation behind clenched teeth, they refuse to let their eyes show uneasiness, they smooth the twitching muscles of the face into an artificial indifference, obeying the dictates of polite conduct. But just because their whole attention is concentrated on controlling the face, the most visible part of the body, they forget their hands, they forget that some people are watching nothing but those hands, guessing from them what the lips curved in a smile, the intentionally indifferent glances wish to conceal. Meanwhile, however, their hands shamelessly reveal their innermost secrets. For a moment inevitably comes when all those carefully controlled, apparently relaxed fingers drop their elegant negligence. In the pregnant moment when the roulette ball drops into its shallow compartment and the winning number is called, in that second every one of those hundred or five hundred hands spontaneously makes a very personal, very individual movement of primitive instinct. And if an observer like me, particularly well-informed as I was because of my husband's hobby, is used to watching the hands perform in this arena, it is more exciting even than music or drama to see so many different temperaments suddenly erupt. I simply cannot tell you how many thousands of varieties of hands there are: wild beasts with hairy, crooked fingers raking in the money like spiders; nervous, trembling hands with pale nails that scarcely dare to touch it; hands noble and vulgar, hands brutal and shy, cunning hands, hands that seem to be stammering—but each of these pairs of hands is different, the expression of an individual life, with the exception of the four or five pairs of hands belonging to the croupiers. Those hands are entirely mechanical, and with their objective, business-like, totally detached precision function like the clicking metal mechanism of a gas meter by comparison with the extreme liveliness of the gamblers' hands. But even those sober hands produce a surprising effect when contrasted with their racing, passionate fellows; you might say they were wearing a different uniform, like policemen in the middle of a surging, agitated riot. And then there is the personal incentive of getting to know the many different habits and passions of individual pairs of hands within a few days; by then I had always made acquaintances among them and divided them, as if they were human beings, into those I liked and those I did not. I found the greed and incivility of some so repulsive that I would always avert my gaze from them, as if from some impropriety. Every new pair of hands to appear on the table, however, was a fresh experience and a source of curiosity to me; I often quite forgot to look at the face which, surrounded by a collar high above them, was set impassively on top of an evening shirt or a glittering décolleté, a cold social mask.

When I entered the gaming hall that evening, passed two crowded tables, reached a third, and was taking out a few coins, I was surprised to hear a very strange sound directly opposite me in the wordless, tense pause that seems to echo with silence and always sets in as the ball, moving sluggishly, hesitates between two numbers. It was a cracking, clicking sound like the snapping of joints. I looked across the table in amazement. And then I saw—I was truly startled!—I saw two hands such as I had never seen before, left and right clutching each other like doggedly determined animals, bracing and extending together and against one another with such heightened tension that the fingers joints cracked with a dry sound like a nut cracking open. They were hands of rare beauty, unusually long, unusually slender, yet taut and muscular—very white, the nails pale at their tips, gently curving and the colour of mother of pearl. I kept watching them all evening, indeed I kept marvelling at those extraordinary, those positively unique hands—but what surprised and alarmed me so much at first was the passion in them, their crazily impassioned expressiveness, the convulsive way they wrestled with and supported each other. I knew at once that I was seeing a human being overflowing with emotion, forcing his passion into his fingertips lest it tear him apart. And then—just as the ball, with a dry click, fell into place in the wheel and the croupier called out the number—at that very moment the two hands suddenly fell apart like a pair of animals struck by a single bullet. They dropped, both of them, truly dead and not just exhausted; they dropped with so graphic an expression of lethargy, disappointment, instant extinction, as if all was finally over, that I can find no words to describe it. For never before or since have I seen such speaking hands, hands in which every muscle was eloquent and passion broke almost tangibly from the pores of the skin. They lay on the green table for a moment like jellyfish cast up by the sea, flat and dead. Then one of them, the right hand, began laboriously raising itself again, beginning with the fingertips; it quivered, drew back, turned on itself, swayed, circled, and suddenly reached nervously for a jetton, rolling the token uncertainly like a little wheel between the tips of thumb and middle finger. And suddenly it arched, like a panther arching its back, and shot forward, positively spitting the hundred-franc jetton out on the middle of the black space. At once, as if at a signal, the inactive, slumbering left hand was seized by excitement too; it rose, slunk, crawled over to its companion hand, which was trembling now as if exhausted by throwing down the jetton, and both hands lay there together trembling, the joints of their fingers working away soundlessly on the table, tapping slightly together like teeth chattering in a fever—no, I had never seen hands of such expressive eloquence, or such spasmodic agitation and tension. Everything else in this vaulted room, the hum from the other halls around it, the calls of the croupiers crying their wares like market traders, the movement of people and of the ball itself which now, dropped from above, was leaping like a thing possessed around the circular cage that was smooth as parquet flooring—all this diversity of whirling, swirling impressions flitting across the nerves suddenly seemed to me dead and dull compared to those two trembling, breathing, gasping, waiting, freezing, trembling hands, that extraordinary pair of hands which somehow held me spellbound.

But finally I could no longer refrain; I had to see the human being, the face to which those magical hands belonged, and fearfully—yes, I do mean fearfully, for I was afraid of those hands!—my gaze slowly travelled up the gambler's sleeves and narrow shoulders. And once again I had a shock, for his face spoke the same fantastically extravagant language of extremes as the hands, shared the same terrible grimness of expression and delicate, almost feminine beauty. I had never seen such a face before, a face so transported and utterly beside itself, and I had plenty of opportunity to observe it at leisure as if it were a mask, an unseeing sculpture: those possessed eyes did not turn to right or left for so much as a second, their pupils were fixed and black beneath the widely opened lids, dead glass balls reflecting that other mahogany-coloured ball rolling and leaping about the roulette wheel in such foolish high spirits. Never, I repeat, had I seen so intense or so fascinating a face. It belonged to a young man of perhaps twenty-four, it was fine-drawn, delicate, rather long and very expressive. Like the hands, it did not seem entirely masculine, but resembled the face of a boy passionately absorbed in a game—although I noticed none of that until later, for now the face was entirely veiled by an expression of greed and of madness breaking out. The thin mouth, thirsting and open, partly revealed the teeth: you could see them ten paces away, grinding feverishly while the parted lips remained rigid. A light blond lock of hair clung damply to his forehead, tumbling forward like the hair of a man falling, and a tic fluttered constantly around his nostrils as if little waves were invisibly rippling beneath the skin. The bowed head was moving instinctively further and further forward; you felt it was being swept away with the whirling of the little ball, and now, for the first time, I understood the convulsive pressure of the hands. Only by the intense strain of pressing them together did the body, falling from its central axis, contrive to keep its balance. I had never—I must repeat it yet again—I had never seen a face in which passion showed so openly, with such shamelessly naked animal feeling, and I stared at that face, as fascinated and spellbound by its obsession as was its own gaze by the leaping, twitching movement of the circling ball. From that moment on I noticed nothing else in the room, everything seemed to me dull, dim and blurred, dark by comparison with the flashing fire of that face, and disregarding everyone else present I spent perhaps an hour watching that one man and every movement he made: the bright light that sparkled in his eyes, the convulsive knot of his hands loosening as if blown apart by an explosion, the parting of the shaking fingers as the croupier pushed twenty gold coins towards their eager grasp. At that moment the face looked suddenly bright and very young, the lines in it smoothed out, the eyes began to gleam, the convulsively bowed body straightened lightly, easily—he suddenly sat there as relaxed as a horseman, borne up by the sense of triumph, fingers toying lovingly, idly with the round coins, clinking them together, making them dance and jingle playfully. Then he turned his head restlessly again, surveyed the green table as if with the flaring nostrils of a young hound seeking the right scent, and suddenly, with one quick movement, placed all the coins on one rectangular space. At once the watchfulness, the tension returned. Once more the little waves, rippling galvanically, spread out from his lips, once again his hands were clasped, the boyish face disappeared behind greedy expectation until the spasmodic tension exploded and fell apart in disappointment: the face that had just looked boyish turned faded, wan and old, light disappeared from the burnt-out eyes, and all this within the space of a second as the ball came to rest on the wrong number. He had lost; he stared at the ball for a few seconds almost like an idiot, as if he did not understand, but as the croupier began calling to whip up interest, his fingers took out a few coins again. But his certainty was gone; first he put the coins on one space, then, thinking better of it, on another, and when the ball had begun to roll his trembling hand, on a sudden impulse, quickly added two crumpled banknotes.

This alternation of up and down, loss and gain, continued without a break for about an hour, and during that hour I did not, even for a moment, take my fascinated gaze from that ever-changing face and all the passions ebbing and flowing over it. I kept my eyes fixed on those magical hands, their every muscle graphically reflecting the whole range of the man's feelings as they rose and fell like a fountain. I had never watched the face of an actor in the theatre as intently as I watched this one, seeing the constant, changing shades of emotion flitting over it like light and shade moving over a landscape. I had never immersed myself so whole-heartedly in a game as I did in the reflection of this stranger's excitement. If someone had been observing me at that moment he would surely have taken my steely gaze for a state of hypnosis, and indeed my benumbed perception was something like that— I simply could not look away from the play of those features, and everything else in the room, the lights, the laughter, the company and its glances, merely drifted vaguely around me, a yellow mist with that face in the middle of it, a flame among flames. I heard nothing, I felt nothing, I did not notice people coming forward beside me, other hands suddenly reaching out like feelers, putting down money or picking it up; I did not see the ball or hear the croupier's voice, yet I saw it all as if I were dreaming, exaggerated as in a concave mirror by the excitement and extravagance of those moving hands. For I did not have to look at the roulette wheel to know whether the ball had come to rest on red or black, whether it was still rolling or beginning to falter. Every stage of the game, loss and gain, hope and disappointment, was fierily reflected in the nerves and movements of that passionate face.

But then came a terrible moment—something that I had been vaguely fearing all this time, something that had weighed like a gathering thunderstorm on my tense nerves, and now suddenly ripped through them. Yet again the ball had fallen back into the shallow depression with that dry little click, yet again came the tense moment when two hundred lips held their breath until the croupier's voice announced the winning number—this time it was zero—while he zealously raked in the clinking coins and crackling notes from all sides. At that moment those two convulsively clasped hands made a particularly terrifying movement, leaping up as if to catch something that wasn't there and then dropping to the table again exhausted, with no strength in them, only the force of gravity flooding back. Then, however, they suddenly came to life yet again, feverishly retreating from the table to the man's own body, clambering up his torso like wild cats, up and down, left and right, nervously trying all his pockets to see if some forgotten coin might not have slipped into one of them. But they always came back empty, and the pointless, useless search began again ever more frantically, while the roulette wheel went on circling and others continued playing, while coins clinked, chairs were shifted on the floor, and all the small sounds, put together a hundredfold, filled the room with a humming note. I trembled, shaking with horror; I felt it all as clearly as if my own fingers were rummaging desperately for a coin in the pockets and folds of my creased garments. And suddenly, with a single abrupt movement, the man rose to his feet opposite me, like a man standing up when he suddenly feels unwell and must rise if he is not to suffocate. His chair crashed to the floor behind him. Without even noticing, without paying any attention to his surprised and abashed neighbours as they avoided his swaying figure, he stumbled away from the table.

The sight petrified me. For I knew at once where the man was going: to his death. A man getting to his feet like that was not on his way back to an inn, a wine bar, a wife, a railway carriage, to any form of life at all, he was plunging straight into the abyss. Even the most hardened spectator in that hellish gaming hall could surely have seen that the man had nothing to fall back on, not at home or in a bank or with a family, but had been sitting here with the last of his money, staking his life, and was now staggering away somewhere else, anywhere, but undoubtedly out of that life. I had feared all along, I had sensed from the first moment, as if by magic, that more than loss or gain was staked on the game, yet now it struck me like a bolt of dark lightning to see the life suddenly go out of his eyes and death cast its pale shadow over his still living face. Instinctively—affected as I was by his own graphic gestures—I clutched at myself while the man tore himself away from his place and staggered out, for his own uncertain gait was now transferred to my own body just as his tension had entered my veins and nerves. Then I was positively wrenched away, I had to follow him; my feet moved without my own volition. It was entirely unconscious, I did not do it of my own accord, it was something happening to me when, taking no notice of anyone, feeling nothing myself, I went out into the corridor leading to the doors.

He was standing at the cloakroom counter, and the attendant had brought him his coat. But his arms would no longer obey him, so the helpful attendant laboriously eased them into the sleeves, as if he were paralysed. I saw him automatically put his hand in his waistcoat pocket to give the man a tip, but his fingers emerged empty. Then he suddenly seemed to remember everything, awkwardly stammered something to the cloakroom attendant, and as before moved forward abruptly and then stumbled like a drunk down the casino steps, where the attendant stood briefly watching him go, with a smile that was at first contemptuous and then understanding.

His bearing shook me so much that I felt ashamed to have seen it. Involuntarily I turned aside, embarrassed to have watched a stranger's despair as if I were in a theatre—but then that vague fear suddenly took me out of myself once again. Quickly, I retrieved my coat, and thinking nothing very definite, purely mechanically and compulsively I hurried out into the dark after the stranger."

Mrs C interrupted her story for a moment. She had been sitting calmly opposite me, speaking almost without a break with her characteristic tranquil objectivity, as only someone who had prepared and carefully organized the events of her tale in advance could speak. Now, for the first time, she stopped, hesitated, and then suddenly broke off and turned directly to me.

"I promised you and myself," she began, rather unevenly, "to tell you all the facts with perfect honesty. Now I must ask you to believe in my honesty, and not assume that my conduct had any ulterior motives. I might not be ashamed of them today, but in this case such suspicions would be entirely unfounded. And I must emphasise that, when I hurried after that ruined gambler in the street, I had certainly not fallen in love with him—I did not think of him as a man at all, and indeed I was over forty myself at the time and had never looked at another man since my husband's death. All that part of my life was finally over; I tell you this explicitly, and I must, or you would not understand the full horror of what happened later. On the other hand, it's true that I would find it difficult to give a clear name to the feeling that drew me so compulsively after the unfortunate man; there was curiosity in it, but above all a dreadful fear, or rather a fear of something dreadful, something I had felt invisibly enveloping the young man like a miasma from the first moment. But such feelings can't be dissected and taken apart, if only because they come over one too compulsively, too fast, too spontaneously—very likely mine expressed nothing but the instinct to help with which one snatches back a child about to run into the road in front of a motor-car. How else can we explain why non-swimmers will jump off a bridge to help a drowning man? They are simply impelled to do it as if by magic, some other will pushes them off the bridge before they have time to consider the pointless bravery of their conduct properly; and in just the same way, without thinking, without conscious reflection, I hurried after the unfortunate young man out of the gaming room, to the casino doors, out of the doors and on to the terrace.

And I am sure that neither you nor any other feeling human being with his eyes open could have withstood that fearful curiosity, for a more disturbing sight can hardly be imagined than the way the gambler, who must have been twenty-four at the most but moved as laboriously as an old man and was swaying like a drunk, dragged himself shakily and disjointedly down the steps to the terrace beside the road. Once there, his body dropped on to a bench, limp as a sack. Again I shuddered as I sensed, from that movement, that the man had reached the end of his tether. Only a dead man or one with nothing left to keep him alive drops like that. His head, fallen to one side, leaned back over the bench, his arms hung limp and shape-less to the ground, and in the dim illumination of the faintly flickering street lights any passer-by would have thought he had been shot. And it was like that—I can't explain why the vision suddenly came into my mind, but all of a sudden it was there, real enough to touch, terrifying and terrible—it was like that, as a man who had been shot, that I saw him before me at that moment, and I knew for certain that he had a revolver in his pocket, and tomorrow he would be found lying lifeless and covered with blood on this or some other bench. For he had dropped like a stone falling into a deep chasm, never to stop until it reaches the bottom: I never saw such a physical expression of exhaustion and despair.

So now, consider my situation: I was standing twenty or thirty paces from the bench and the motionless, broken man on it, with no idea what to do, on the one hand wishing to help, on the other restrained by my innate and inbred reluctance to speak to a strange man in the street. The gaslights flickered dimly in the overcast sky, few figures hurried past, for it was nearly midnight and I was almost entirely alone in the park with this suicidal figure. Five or ten times I had already pulled myself together and approached him, but shame or perhaps that deeper premonitory instinct, the idea that falling men are likely to pull those who come to their aid down with them, made me withdraw—and in this midst of this indecision I was clearly aware of the pointless, ridiculous aspect of the situation. None the less, I could neither speak nor turn away, I could not do anything but I could not leave him. And I hope you will believe me when I say that for perhaps an hour, an endless hour, I walked indecisively up and down that terrace, while time was divided up by thousands of little sounds from the breaking waves of the invisible sea—so shaken and transfixed was I by the idea of the annihilation of a human being.

Yet I could not summon up the courage to say a word or make a move, and I would have waited like that half the night, or perhaps in the end my wiser self-interest would have prevailed on me to go home, and indeed I think I had already made up my mind to leave that helpless bundle of misery lying there—when a superior force put an end to my indecision. It began to rain. All evening the wind had been piling up heavy spring clouds full of moisture above the sea, lungs and heart felt the pressure of the lowering sky, and now drops suddenly began to splash down. Soon a heavy rain was falling in wet torrents blown about by the wind. I instinctively sheltered under the projecting roof of a kiosk, but although I put up my umbrella gusts of wind kept blowing the rain on my dress. I felt the cold mist thrown up by the falling raindrops spray my face and hands.

But—and it was such a terrible sight that even now, two decades later, the memory still constricts my throat—but in the middle of this cloudburst the unfortunate man stayed perfectly still on his bench, never moving. Water was gurgling and dripping from all the eaves; you could hear the rumble of carriages from the city; people with their coat collars turned up hurried past to right and to left; all living creatures ducked in alarm, fled, ran, sought shelter, man and beast felt universal fear of the torrential element—but that black heap of humanity on the bench did not stir or move. I told you before that he had the magical gift of graphically expressing everything he felt in movement and gesture. But nothing, nothing on earth could convey despair, total self-surrender, death in the midst of life to such shattering effect as his immobility, the way he sat there in the falling rain, not moving, feeling nothing, too tired to rise and walk the few steps to the shelter of the projecting roof, utterly indifferent to his own existence. No sculptor, no poet, not Michelangelo or Dante has ever brought that sense of ultimate despair, of ultimate human misery so feelingly to my mind as the sight of that living figure letting the watery element drench him, too weary and uncaring to make a single move to protect himself.

That made me act; I couldn't help it. Pulling myself together, I ran the gauntlet of the lashing rain and shook the dripping bundle of humanity to make him get up from the bench. 'Come along!' I seized his arm. Something stared up at me, with difficulty. Something in him seemed to be slowly preparing to move, but he did not understand. 'Come along!' Once again, almost angry now, I tugged at his wet sleeve. Then he slowly stood up, devoid of will and swaying. 'What do you want?' he asked, and I could not reply, for I myself had no idea where to take him—just away from the cold downpour where he had been sitting so senselessly, suicidally, in the grip of deep despair. I did not let go of his arm but dragged the man on, since he had no will of his own, to the sales kiosk where the narrow, projecting roof at least partly sheltered him from the raging attack of the stormy rain as the wind tossed it wildly back and forth. That was all I wanted, I had nothing else in mind, just to get him somewhere dry, under a roof. As yet I had thought no further.

So we stood side by side on that narrow strip of dry ground, the wall of the kiosk behind us and above us only the roof, which was not large enough, for the insatiable rain insidiously came in under it as sudden gusts of wind flung wet, chilly showers over our clothes and into our faces. The situation became intolerable. I could hardly stand there any longer beside this dripping wet stranger. On the other hand, having dragged him over here I couldn't just leave him and walk away without a word. Something had to be done, and gradually I forced myself to think clearly. It would be best, I thought, to send him home in a cab and then go home myself; he would be able to look after himself tomorrow. So as he stood beside me gazing fixedly out at the turbulent night I asked, 'Where do you live?'

'I'm not staying anywhere ... I only arrived from Nice this morning ... we can't go to my place.'

I did not immediately understand this last remark. Only later did I realise that the man took me for ... for a *demi-mondaine*, one of the many women who haunt the casino by night, hoping to extract a little money from lucky gamblers or drunks. After all, what else was he to think, for only now that I tell you about it do I feel all the improbability, indeed the fantastic nature of my situation—what else was he to think of me? The way I had pulled him off the bench and dragged him away as if it were perfectly natural was certainly not the conduct of a lady. But this idea did not occur to me at once. Only later, only too late did his terrible misapprehension dawn upon me, or I would never have said what I did next, in words that were bound to reinforce his impression. 'Then we'll just take a room in a hotel. You can't stay here. You must get under cover somewhere.'

Now I understood his painful misunderstanding, for he did not turn towards me but merely rejected the idea with a certain contempt in his voice: 'I don't need a room; I don't need anything now. Don't bother, you won't get anything out of me. You've picked the wrong man. I have no money.'

This too was said in a dreadful tone, with shattering indifference, and the way he stood there dripping wet and leaning against the wall, slack and exhausted to the bone, shook me so much that I had no time to waste on taking petty offence. I merely sensed, as I had from the first moment when I saw him stagger from the gaming hall, as I had felt all through this improbable hour, that here was a human being, a young, living, breathing human being on the very brink of death, and I must save him. I came closer.

'Never mind money, come along! You can't stay here. I'll get you under cover. Don't worry about anything, just come with me.'

He turned his head and I felt, while the rain drummed round us with a hollow sound and the eaves cast water down to splash at our feet, that for the first time he was trying to make out my face in the dark. His body seemed to be slowly shaking off its lethargy too.

'As you like,' he said, giving in. 'It's all one to me ... after all, why not? Let's go.' I put up my umbrella, he moved to my side and took my arm. I felt this sudden intimacy uncomfortable; indeed, it horrified me. I was alarmed to the depths of my heart. But I did not feel bold enough to ask him to refrain, for if I rejected him now he would fall into the bottomless abyss, and everything I had tried to do so far would be in vain. We walked the few steps back to the casino, and only now did it strike me

41

that I had no idea what to do with him. I had better take him to a hotel, I thought quickly, and give him money to spend the night there and go home in the morning. I was not thinking beyond that. And as the carriages were now rapidly drawing up outside the casino I hailed a cab and we got in. When the driver asked where to, I couldn't think what to say at first. But realising that the drenched, dripping man beside me would not be welcome in any of the best hotels—on the other hand, genuinely inexperienced as I was, with nothing else in mind—I just told the cabby, 'Some simple hotel, anywhere!'

The driver, indifferent, and wet with rain himself, drove his horses on. The stranger beside me said not a word, the wheels rattled, the rain splashed heavily against the windows, and I felt as if I were travelling with a corpse in that dark, lightless rectangular space, in a vehicle like a coffin. I tried to think of something to say to relieve the strange, silent horror of our presence there together, but I could think of nothing. After a few minutes the cab stopped. I got out first and paid the driver, who shut the door after us as if drunk with sleep. We were at the door of a small hotel that was unknown to me, with a glass porch above us providing a tiny area of shelter from the rain, which was still lashing the impenetrable night around us with ghastly monotony.

The stranger, giving way to his inertia, had instinctively leaned against the wall, and water was dripping from his wet hat and crumpled garments. He stood there like a drunk who has been fished out of the river, still dazed, and a channel of water trickling down from him formed around the small patch of ground where he stood. But he made not the slightest effort to shake himself or take off the hat from which raindrops kept running over his forehead and face. He stood there entirely apathetically, and I cannot tell you how his broken demeanour moved me.

But something had to be done. I put my hand into my bag.

'Here are a hundred francs,' I said. 'Take a room and go back to Nice tomorrow.'

He looked up in astonishment.

'I was watching you in the gaming hall,' I continued urgently, noticing his hesitation. 'I know you've lost everything, and I fear you're well on the way to doing something stupid. There's no shame in accepting help—here, take it!'

But he pushed away my hand with an energy I wouldn't have expected in him. 'You are very good,' he said, 'but don't waste your money. There's no help for me now. Whether I sleep tonight or not makes not the slightest difference. It will all be over tomorrow anyway. There's no help for me.'

'No, you must take it,' I urged. 'You'll see things differently tomorrow. Go upstairs and sleep on it. Everything will look different in daylight.'

But when I tried to press the money on him again he pushed my hand away almost violently. 'Don't,' he repeated dully. 'There's no point in it. Better to do it out of doors than leave blood all over their room here. A hundred or even a thousand francs won't help me. I'd just go to the gaming hall again tomorrow with the last few francs, and I wouldn't stop until they were all gone. Why begin again? I've had enough.'

You have no idea how that dull tone of voice went to my heart, but think of it: a couple of inches from you stands a young, bright, living, breathing human being, and you know that if you don't do your utmost, then in a few hours time this thinking, speaking, breathing specimen of youth will be a corpse. And now I felt a desire like rage, like fury, to overcome his senseless resistance. I grasped his arm. 'That's enough stupid talk. You go up these steps now and take a room, and I'll come in the morning and take you to the station. You must get away from here, you must go home tomorrow, and I won't rest until I've seen you sitting in the train with a ticket. You can't throw your life away so young just because you've lost a couple of hundred francs, or a couple of thousand. That's cowardice, silly hysteria concocted from anger and bitterness. You'll see that I'm right tomorrow!'

'Tomorrow!' he repeated in a curiously gloomy, ironic tone. 'Tomorrow! If you knew where I'd be tomorrow! I wish I knew myself—I'm mildly curious to find out. No, go home, my dear, don't bother about me and don't waste your money.'

But I wasn't giving up now. It had become like a mania obsessing me. I took his hand by force and pressed the banknote into it. 'You will take this money and go in at once!' And so saying I stepped firmly up to the door and rang the bell. 'There, now I've rung, and the porter will be here in a minute. Go in and lie down. I'll be outside here at nine tomorrow to take you straight to the station. Don't worry about anything, I'll see to what's necessary to get you home. But now go to bed, have a good sleep, and don't think of anything else!'

At that moment the key turned inside the door and the porter opened it.

'Come on, then!' said my companion suddenly, in a harsh, firm embittered voice, and I felt his fingers span my wrist in an iron grip. I was alarmed ... so greatly alarmed, so paralysed, struck as if by lightning, that all my composure vanished. I wanted to resist, tear myself away, but my will seemed numbed, and I ... well, you will understand ... I was ashamed to struggle with a stranger in front of the porter, who stood there waiting impatiently. And so, suddenly, I was inside the hotel. I wanted to speak, say something, but my throat would not obey me ... and his hand lay heavy and commanding on my arm. I vaguely felt it draw me as if unawares up a flight of steps—a key clicked in a lock. And suddenly I was alone with this stranger in a strange room, in some hotel whose name I do not know to this day."

Mrs C stopped again, and suddenly rose to her feet. It seemed that her voice would not obey her any more. She went over to the window and looked out in silence for some minutes, or perhaps she was just resting her forehead on the cold pane; I did not have the courage to look closely, for I found it painful to see the old lady so agitated. So I sat quite still, asking no questions, making no sound, and waited until she came back, stepping firmly, and sat down opposite me.

"Well—now the most difficult part is told. And I hope you will believe me when I assure you yet again, when I swear by all that is sacred to me, by my honour and my children, that up to that moment no idea of any ... any relationship with the stranger had entered my mind, that I really had been suddenly plunged into this situation against my own will, indeed entirely unawares, as if I had fallen through a trapdoor from the level path of my existence. I have promised to be honest with you and with myself, so I repeat again that I embarked on this tragic venture merely through a rather overwrought desire to help, not through any other, any personal feeling, quite without any wishes or forebodings.

You must spare me the tale of what happened in that room that night; I myself have forgotten not a moment of it, and I never will. I spent it wrestling with another human being for his life, and I repeat, it was a battle of life and death. I felt only too clearly, with every fibre of my being, that this stranger, already half-lost, was clutching at his last chance with all the avid passion of a man threatened by death. He clung to me like one who already feels the abyss yawning beneath him. For my part, I summoned everything in me to save him by all the means at my command. A human being may know such an hour perhaps only once in his life, and out of millions, again, perhaps only one will know it—but for that terrible chance I myself would never have guessed how ardently, desperately, with what boundless greed a man given up for lost will still suck at every red drop of life. Kept safe for twenty years from all the demonic forces of existence, I would never have understood how magnificently, how fantastically Nature can merge hot and cold, life and death, delight and despair together in a few brief moments. And that night was so full of conflict and of talk, of passion and anger and hatred, with tears of entreaty and intoxication, that it seemed to me to last a thousand years, and we two human beings who fell entwined into its chasm, one of us in frenzy, the other unsuspecting, emerged from that mortal tumult changed, completely transformed, senses and emotions transmuted.

But I don't want to talk about that. I cannot and will not describe it. However, I must just tell you of the extraordinary moment when I woke in the morning from a leaden sleep, from nocturnal depths such as I had never known before. It took me a long time to open my eyes, and the first thing I saw was a strange ceiling over me, and then, looking further an entirely strange, unknown, ugly room. I had no idea how I came to be there. At first I told myself I must still be dreaming, an unusually lucid, transparent dream into which I had passed from my dull, confused slumber—but the sparkling bright sunshine outside the windows was unmistakably genuine, the light of morning, and the sounds of the street echoed from below, the rattle of carriages, the ringing of tram bells, the noise of people—so now I knew that I was awake and not dreaming. I instinctively sat up to get my bearings, and then—as my glance moved sideways—then I saw, and I can never describe my alarm to you, I saw a stranger sleeping in the broad bed beside me ... a strange, perfectly strange, half-naked, unknown man ... oh, I know there's no real way to describe the awful realisation; it struck me with such terrible force that I sank back powerless. But not in a kindly faint, not falling unconscious, far from it: with lightning speed, everything became as clear to me as it was inexplicable, and all I wanted was to die of revulsion and shame at suddenly finding myself in an unfamiliar bed in a decidedly shady hotel, with a complete stranger beside me. I still remember how my heart missed a beat, how I held my breath as if that would extinguish my life and above all my consciousness, which grasped everything yet understood none of it.

I shall never know how long I lay like that, all my limbs icy cold: the dead must lie rigid in their coffins in much the same way. All I know is that I had closed my eyes and was praying to God, to some heavenly power, that this might not be true, might not be real. But my sharpened senses would not let me deceive myself, I could hear people talking in the next room, water running, footsteps shuffling along the corridor outside, and each of these signs mercilessly proved that my senses were terribly alert.

How long this dreadful condition lasted I cannot say: such moments are outside the measured time of ordinary life. But suddenly another fear came over me, swift and terrible: the stranger whose name I did not know might wake up and speak to me. And I knew at once there was only one thing to do: I must get dressed and make my escape before he woke. I must not let him set eyes on me again, I must not speak to him again. I must save myself before it was too late, go away, away, away, back to some kind of life of my own, to my hotel, I must leave this pernicious place, leave this country, never meet him again, never look him in the eye, have no witnesses, no accusers, no one who knew. The idea dispelled my faintness: very cautiously, with the furtive movements of a thief, I inched out of bed (for I was desperate to make no noise) and groped my way over to my clothes. I dressed very carefully, trembling all the time lest he might wake up, and then I had finished, I had done it. Only my hat lay at the foot of the bed on the far side of the room, and then, as I tiptoed over to pick it up—I couldn't help it, at that moment I had to cast another glance at the face of the stranger who had fallen into my life like a stone dropping off a

window-sill. I meant it to be just one glance, but it was curious—the strange young man who lay sleeping there really was
a stranger to me. At first I did not recognise his face from yesterday. The impassioned, tense, desperately distressed features
of the mortally agitated man might have been entirely extinguished—this man's face was not the same, but was an utterly
childlike, utterly boyish face that positively radiated purity and
cheerfulness. The lips, so grim yesterday as he clenched his teeth
on them, were dreaming, had fallen softly apart, half curving
in a smile; the fair hair curled gently over the smooth forehead,
the breath passed from his chest over his body at repose like the
mild rippling of waves.

Perhaps you may remember that I told you earlier I had
never before seen greed and passion expressed with such outrageous extravagance by any human being as by that stranger
at the gaming table. And I tell you now that I had never, even
in children whose baby slumbers sometimes cast an angelic
aura of cheerfulness around them, seen such an expression of
brightness, of truly blissful sleep. The uniquely graphic nature
of that face showed all its feelings, at present the paradisial easing of all internal heaviness, a sense of freedom and salvation.
At this surprising sight all my own fear and horror fell from
me like a heavy black cloak—I was no longer ashamed, no, I
was almost glad. The terrible and incomprehensible thing that
had happened suddenly made sense to me; I was happy, I was
proud to think that but for my dedicated efforts the beautiful,
delicate young man lying here carefree and quiet as a flower
would have been found somewhere on a rocky slope, his body
shattered and bloody, his face ruined, lifeless, with staring eyes.
I had saved him; he was safe. And now I looked—I cannot put it
any other way—I looked with maternal feeling at the man I had
reborn into life more painfully than I bore my own children.
In the middle of that shabby, threadbare room in a distasteful,
grubby house of assignation, I was overcome by the kind of

emotion—ridiculous as you may find it put into words—the kind of emotion one might have in church, a rapturous sense of wonder and sanctification. From the most dreadful moment of a whole life there now grew a second life, amazing and overwhelming, coming in sisterly fashion to meet me.

Had I made too much noise moving about? Had I involuntarily exclaimed out loud? I don't know, but suddenly the sleeping man opened his eyes. I flinched back in alarm. He looked round in surprise—just as I had done before earlier, and now he in his own turn seemed to be emerging with difficulty from great depths of confusion. His gaze wandered intently round the strange, unfamiliar room and then fell on me in amazement. But before he spoke, or could quite pull himself together, I had control of myself. I did not let him say a word, I allowed no questions, no confidences; nothing of yesterday or of last night was to be explained, discussed or mulled over again.

'I have to go now,' I told him quickly. 'You stay here and get dressed. I'll meet you at twelve at the entrance to the casino, and I'll take care of everything else.'

And before he could say a word in reply I fled, to be rid of the sight of the room, and without turning back left the hotel whose name I did not know, any more than I knew the name of the stranger with whom I had just spent the night."

Mrs C interrupted her narrative for a moment again, but all the strain and distress had gone from her voice: like a carriage that toils uphill with difficulty but then, having reached the top, rolls swiftly and smoothly down the other side, her account now proceeded more easily:

"Well—so I made haste to my hotel through the morning light of the streets. The drop in the temperature had driven all the hazy mists from the sky above, just as my own distress had been dispelled. For remember what I told you earlier: I had given up my own life entirely after my husband's death. My children did not need me, I didn't care for my own company, and there's no point in a life lived aimlessly. Now, for the first time, a task had suddenly come my way: I had saved a human being, I had exerted all my powers to snatch him back from destruction. There was only a little left to do—for my task must be completed to the end. So I entered my hotel, ignoring the porter's surprise when he saw me returning at nine in the morning—no shame and chagrin over last night's events oppressed me now, I felt my will to live suddenly revive, and an unexpectedly new sense of the point of my existence flowed warmly through my veins. Once in my room I quickly changed my clothes, putting my mourning aside without thinking (as I noticed only later) and choosing a lighter colour instead, went to the bank to withdraw money, and made haste to the station to find out train times. With a determination that surprised me I also made a few other arrangements. Now there was nothing left to do but ensure the departure from Monte Carlo and ultimate salvation of the man whom fate had cast in my way.

It is true that I needed strength to face him personally. Everything yesterday had taken place in the dark, in a vortex; we had been like two stones thrown out of a torrential stream suddenly striking together; we scarcely knew each other face to face, and I wasn't even sure whether the stranger would recognise me again. Yesterday had been chance, frenzy, a case of two confused people possessed; today I must be more open with him, since I must now confront him in the pitiless light of day with myself, my own face, as a living human being.

But it all turned out much easier than I expected. No sooner had I approached the casino at the appointed hour than a young man jumped up from a bench and made haste towards me. There was something so spontaneous, so child-like, unplanned and happy in his surprise and in each of his eloquent movements; he almost flew to me, the radiance of a joy that was both grateful and deferential in his eyes, which were lowered humbly as soon as they felt my confusion in his presence. Gratitude is so seldom found, and those who are most grateful cannot express it, are silent in their confusion, or ashamed, or sometimes seem ungracious just to conceal their feelings. But in this man, the expression of whose every feeling God, like a mysterious sculptor, had made sensual, beautiful, graphic, his gratitude glowed with radiant passion right through his body. He bent over my hand and remained like that for a moment, the narrow line of his boyish head reverently bowed, respectfully brushing kisses on my fingers; only then did he step back, asked how I was, and looked at me most movingly. There was such courtesy in everything he said that within a few minutes the last of my anxiety had gone. As if reflecting the lightening of my own feelings, the landscape around was shining, the spell on it broken: the sea that had been disturbed and angry yesterday lay so calm and bright that every pebble beneath the gently breaking surf gleamed white, and the casino, that den of iniquity, looked up with Moorish brightness to the damask sky that was now swept clean. The kiosk with the projecting roof beneath which the pouring rain had forced us to shelter yesterday proved to be a flower stall; great bunches of flowers and foliage lay there in motley confusion, in white, red, other bright colours and green, and a young girl in a colourful blouse was offering them for sale.

I invited him to lunch with me in a small restaurant, and there the young stranger told me the story of his tragic venture. It confirmed my first presentiment when I had seen his trembling, nervously shaking hands on the green the table. He came from an old aristocratic family in the Austrian part of Poland, was destined for a diplomatic career, had studied in Vienna and passed his first examination with great success a month ago. As a reward, and to celebrate the occasion, his uncle, a high-ranking general-staff officer, had taken him to the Prater in a cab, and they went to the races. His uncle was lucky with his bets and won three times running; then they ate supper in an elegant restaurant on the strength of the fat wad of banknotes that were the uncle's gains. Next day, again to mark his success in the examinations, the budding diplomat received a sum of money from his father which was as much as his usual monthly allowance. Two days earlier this would have seemed to him a large sum, but now, seeing how easily his uncle had won money, it struck him as trifling and left him indifferent. Directly after dinner, therefore, he went to the races again, laid wild, frenzied bets, and fortune—or rather misfortune—would have it that he left the Prater after the last race with three times the sum he had brought there. Now a mania for gambling infected him; sometimes he went to the races, sometimes to play in coffee-houses and clubs, exhausting his time, his studies, his nerves, and above all his money. He was no longer able to think or to sleep peacefully, and he was quite unable to control himself; one night, coming home from a club where he had lost everything, he found a crumpled banknote forgotten in his waistcoat pocket as he was undressing. There was no holding him; he got dressed again and walked the streets until he found a few people playing dominoes in a coffee-house, and sat with them until dawn. On one occasion his married sister came to his aid, paying his debts to money-lenders who were very ready to give credit to the heir of a great and noble name. For a while he was lucky at play again—but then matters went inexorably downhill, and the more he lost, the more urgently did unsecured obligations and fixed-term IOUs require him to find relief by winning. He had long ago pawned his watch and his clothes, and at last a terrible thing happened: he stole two large pearl earrings that she seldom wore from his old aunt's dressing-table. He pawned one of the pearls for a large sum, which his gambling quadrupled that evening. But instead of redeeming the pearl he staked all his winnings and lost. At the time when he left Vienna the theft had not yet been discovered, so he pawned the second pearl and on a sudden impulse travelled by train to Monte Carlo to win the fortune he dreamed of at roulette. On arrival he had sold his suitcase, his clothes, his umbrella; he had nothing left but a revolver with four cartridges, and a small cross set with jewels given him by his godmother, Princess X. He did not want to part with the cross, but it too had been sold for fifty francs that afternoon, just to let him try to satisfy his urge by playing for life or death one last time that evening.

He told me all this with the captivating charm of his original and lively nature. And I listened shaken, gripped and much moved, but not for a moment did it occur to me to feel horror that the man at my table was in sober fact a thief. Yesterday, if someone had so much as suggested to me that I, a woman with a blameless past who expected the company she kept to be strictly and conventionally virtuous, would be sitting here on familiar terms with a perfectly strange young man, not much older than my son, who had stolen a pair of pearl earrings, I would have thought he had taken leave of his senses and such a thing was impossible. But I felt no horror at all as he told his tale, for he spoke so naturally and passionately that it seemed more like the account of a fever or illness than a crime. Moreover, the word 'impossible' had suddenly lost its meaning for a woman who had known such an unexpected, torrential experience as I had the night before. In those ten hours, I had come to know immeasurably more about reality than in my preceding forty respectable years of life.

Yet something else about his confession did alarm me, and that was the feverish glint in his eyes, which made all the nerves of his face twitch galvanically as he talked about his passion for gambling. Even speaking of it aroused him, and his face graphically and with terrible clarity illustrated that tension between pleasure and torment. His hands, those beautiful, nervous, slender-jointed hands, instinctively began to turn into preying, hunting, fleeing animal creatures again, just as they did at the gaming table. As he spoke I saw them suddenly trembling, beginning at the wrists, arching and clenching into fists, then opening up to intertwine their fingers once more. And when he confessed to the theft of the pearl earrings they suddenly performed a swift, leaping, quick, thieving movement—I involuntarily jumped. I could see his fingers pouncing on the jewels and swiftly stowing them away in the hollow of his clenched hand. And with nameless horror, I recognised that the very last drop of this man's blood was poisoned by his addiction.

That was the one thing that so shattered and horrified me about his tale, the pitiful enslavement of a young, light-hearted, naturally carefree man to a mad passion. I considered it my prime duty to persuade my unexpected protégé, in friendly fashion, that he must leave Monte Carlo, where the temptation was most dangerous, without delay; he must return to his family this very day, before anyone noticed that the pearl earrings were gone and his future was ruined for ever. I promised him money for his journey and to redeem the jewellery, though only on condition that he left today and swore to me, on his honour, never to touch a card or play any other game of chance again.

I shall never forget the passion of gratitude, humble at first, then gradually more ardent, with which that lost stranger listened to me, how he positively drank in my words as I promised him help, and then he suddenly reached both hands over the table to take mine in a gesture I can never forget, a gesture of what one might call adoration and sacred promise. There were tears in his bright but slightly confused eyes; his whole body was trembling nervously with happy excitement. I have tried to describe the uniquely expressive quality of his gestures to you several times already, but I cannot depict this one, for

it conveyed ecstatic, supernal delight such as a human countenance seldom turns on us, comparable only to that white shade
in which, waking from a dream, we think we see the countenance of an angel vanishing.

Why conceal it? I could not withstand that glance. Gratitude
is delightful because it is so seldom found, tender feeling does
one good, and such exuberance was delightfully new and
heart-warming to me, sober, cool woman that I was. And with
that crushed, distressed young man, the landscape itself had
revived as if by magic after last night's rain. The sea, calm as
a millpond, lay shining blue beneath the sky as we came out
of the restaurant, and the only white to be seen was the white
of seagulls swooping in that other, celestial blue. You know
the Riviera landscape. It is always beautiful, but offers its rich
colours to the eye in leisurely fashion, flat as a picture postcard,
a lethargic sleeping beauty who admits all glances, imperturb-
able and almost oriental in her ever-opulent willingness. But
sometimes, very occasionally, there are days when this beauty
rises up, breaks out, cries out loud, you might say, with gaudy,
fanatically sparkling colours, triumphantly flinging her flower-
like brightness in your face, glowing, burning with sensuality.
And the stormy chaos of the night before had turned to such
a lively day, the road was washed white, the sky was turquoise,
and everywhere bushes ignited like colourful torches among
the lush, drenched green foliage. The mountains seemed suddenly lighter and closer in the cooler, sunny air, as if they were
crowding towards the gleaming, polished little town out of
curiosity. Stepping outside, you sensed at every glance the
challenging, cheering aspect of Nature spontaneously drawing your heart to her. 'Let's hire a carriage and drive along the
Corniche,' I said.

The young man nodded enthusiastically: he seemed to be
really seeing and noticing the landscape for the first time since
his arrival. All he had seen so far was the dank casino hall

with its sultry, sweaty smell, its crowds of ugly visitors with their twisted features, and a rough, grey, clamorous sea outside. But now the sunny beach lay spread out before us like a huge fan, and the eye leaped with pleasure from one distant point to another. We drove along the beautiful road in a slow carriage (this was before the days of the motor-car), past many villas and many fine views; a hundred times, seeing every house, every villa in the green shade of the pine trees, one felt a secret wish to live there, quiet and content, away from the world!

Was I ever happier in my life than in that hour? I don't know. Beside me in the carriage sat the young man who had been a prey to death and disaster yesterday and now, in amazement, stood in the spray of the sparkling white dome of the sun above; years seemed to have dropped away from him. He had become all boy, a handsome, sportive child with a playful yet respectful look in his eyes, and nothing about him delighted me more than his considerate attentiveness. If the carriage was going up a steep climb which the horses found arduous, he jumped nimbly down to push from behind. If I named a flower or pointed to one by the roadside, he hurried to pluck it. He picked up a little toad that was hopping with difficulty along the road, lured out by last night's rain, and carried it carefully over to the green grass, where it would not be crushed as the carriage went by; and from time to time, in great high spirits, he would say the most delightful and amusing things; I believe he found laughter of that kind a safety valve, and without it he would have had to sing or dance or fool around in some way, so happily inebriated was the expression of his sudden exuberance.

As we were driving slowly through a tiny village high up on the road, he suddenly raised his hat politely. I was surprised and asked who he was greeting, since he was a stranger among strangers here. He flushed slightly at my question and explained, almost apologetically, that we had just passed a church, and at home in Poland, as in all strict Catholic countries, it was usual from childhood on to raise your hat outside any church or other place of worship. I was deeply moved by this exquisite respect for religion, and remembering the cross he had mentioned, I asked if he was a devout believer. When he modestly confessed, with a touch of embarrassment, that he hoped to be granted God's grace, an idea suddenly came to me. 'Stop!' I told the driver, and quickly climbed out of the carriage. He followed me in surprise, asking, 'Where are we going?' I said only, 'Come with me.'

In his company I went back to the church, a small country church built of brick. The interior looked chalky, grey and empty; the door stood open, so that a yellow beam of light cut sharply through the dark, where blue shadows surrounded a small altar. Two candles, like veiled eyes, looked out of the warm, incense-scented twilight. We entered, he took off his hat, dipped his hand in the basin of holy water, crossed himself and genuflected. When he was standing again I took his arm. 'Go and find an altar or some image here that is holy to you,' I urged him, 'and swear the oath I will recite to you.' He looked at me in surprise, almost in alarm. But quickly understanding, he went over to a niche, made the sign of the cross and obediently knelt down. 'Say after me,' I said, trembling with excitement myself, 'say after me: I swear ... '—'I swear,' he repeated, and I continued, 'that I will never play for money again, whatever the game may be, I swear that I will never again expose my life and my honour to the dangers of that passion.'

He repeated the words, trembling: they lingered loud and clear in the empty interior. Then it was quiet for a moment, so quiet that you could hear the faint rustling of the trees outside as the wind blew through their leaves. Suddenly he threw himself down like a penitent and, in tones of ecstasy such as I had never heard before, poured out a flood of rapid, confused words in Polish. I did not understand what he was saying, but it was obviously an ecstatic prayer, a prayer of gratitude and remorse, for in his stormy confession he kept bowing his head humbly down on the prayer desk, repeating the strange sounds ever more passionately, and uttering the same word more and more violently and with extraordinary ardour. I have never heard prayer like that before or since, in any church in the world. As he prayed his hands clung convulsively to the wooden prayer desk, his whole body shaken by an internal storm that sometimes caught him up and sometimes cast him down again. He saw and felt nothing else: his whole being seemed to exist in another world, in a purgatorial fire of transmutation, or rising to a holier sphere. At last he slowly stood up, made the sign of the cross, and turned with an effort. His knees were trembling, his countenance was pale as the face of a man exhausted. But when he saw me his eyes beamed, a pure, a truly devout smile lit up his ecstatic face; he came closer, bowed low in the Russian manner, took both my hands and touched them reverently with his lips. 'God has sent you to me. I was thanking him.' I did not know what to say, but I could have wished the organ to crash out suddenly above the low pews, for I felt that I had succeeded: I had saved this man for ever.

We emerged from the church into the radiant, flooding light of that May-like day; the world had never before seemed to me more beautiful. Then we drove slowly on in the carriage for another two hours, taking the panoramic road over the hills which offers a new view at every turn. But we spoke no more. After so much emotion, any other words would have seemed an anti-climax. And when by chance my eyes met his, I had to turn them away as if ashamed, so shaken was I by the sight of my own miracle.

We returned to Monte Carlo at about five in the afternoon. I had an appointment with relatives which I could not cancel at this late date. And in fact I secretly wished for a pause in which to recover from feelings that had been too violently aroused. For this was too much happiness. I felt that I must rest from my overheated, ecstatic condition. I had never known anything like it in my life before. So I asked my protégé to come into my hotel with me for a moment, and there in my room I gave him the money for his journey and to redeem the jewellery. We agreed that while I kept my appointment he would go and buy his ticket, and then we would meet at seven in the entrance hall of the station, half an hour before the departure of the train taking him home by way of Genoa. When I was about to give him the five banknotes his lips turned curiously pale. 'No ... no money ... I beg you, not money!' he uttered through his teeth, while his agitated fingers quivered nervously. 'No money ... not money ... I can't stand the sight of it!' he repeated, as if physically over-come by nausea or fear. But I soothed him, saying it was only a loan, and if he felt troubled by it then he could give me a receipt. 'Yes, yes ... a receipt,' he murmured, looking away, cramming the crumpled notes into his pocket without looking at them, like something sticky that soiled his fingers, and he scribbled a couple of words on a piece of paper in swift, flying characters. When he looked up damp sweat was standing out on his brow; something within seemed to be choking him, and no sooner had he given me the note than an impulse seemed to pass through him and suddenly—I was so startled that I instinctively flinched back—suddenly he fell on his knees and kissed the hem of my dress. It was an indescribable gesture; its overwhelming vio-lence made me tremble all over. A strange shuddering came over me; I was confused, and could only stammer, 'Thank you for showing your gratitude—but do please go now! We'll say goodbye at seven in the station hall.'

He looked at me with a gleam of emotion moistening his eye; for a moment I thought he was going to say something, for a moment it seemed as if he were coming towards me. But then he suddenly bowed deeply again, very deeply, and left the room."

Once again Mrs C interrupted her story. She had risen and gone to the window to look out, and she stood there motionless for a long time. Watching the silhouette of her back, I saw it shiver slightly, and she swayed. All at once she turned back to me with determination, and her hands, until now calm and at rest, suddenly made a violent, tearing movement as if to rip something apart. Then she looked at me with a hard, almost defiant glance, and abruptly began again.

"I promised to be completely honest with you, and now I see how necessary that promise was. For only now that, for the first time, I make myself describe the whole course of those hours exactly as they happened, seeking words for what was a very complicated, confused feeling, only now do I clearly understand much that I did not know at the time, or perhaps would not acknowledge. So I will be firm and will not spare myself, and I will tell you the truth too: then, at the moment when the young man left the room and I remained there alone, I felt—it was a dazed sensation, like swooning—I felt a hard blow strike my heart. Something had hurt me mortally, but I did not know, or refused to know, what, after all, it was in my protégé's touchingly respectful conduct that wounded me so painfully.

But now that I force myself to bring up all the past unsparingly, in proper order, as if it were strange to me, and your presence as a witness allows no pretence, no craven concealment of a feeling which shames me, I clearly see that what hurt so much at the time was disappointment ... my disappointment that ... that the young man had gone away so obediently ... that he did not try to detain me, to stay with me. It was because he humbly and respectfully fell in with my first attempt to persuade him to leave, instead ... instead of trying to take me in his arms. It was because he merely revered me as a saint who had appeared to him along his way and did not ... did not feel for me as a woman.

That was the disappointment I felt, a disappointment I did not admit to myself either then or later, but a woman's feelings know everything without words, without conscious awareness. For—and now I will deceive myself no longer—for if he had embraced me then, if he had asked me then, I would have gone to the ends of the earth with him, I would have dishonoured my name and the name of my children—I would have eloped with him, caring nothing for what people would say or the dictates of my own reason, just as Madame Henriette ran off with the young Frenchman whom she hadn't even met the day before. I wouldn't have asked where we were going, or how long it would last, I wouldn't have turned to look back at my previous life—I would have sacrificed my money, my name, my fortune and my honour to him, I would have begged in the street for him, there is probably no base conduct in the world to which he could not have brought me. I would have thrown away all that we call modesty and reason if he had only spoken one word, taken one step towards me, if he had tried to touch me—so lost in him was I at that moment. But ... as I told you ... the young man, in his strangely dazed condition, did not spare another glance for me and the woman in me ... and I knew how much, how fervently I longed for him only when I was alone again, when the passion that had just been lighting up his radiant, his positively seraphic face was cast darkly back on me and now lingered in the void of an abandoned breast. With difficulty, I pulled myself together. My appointment was a doubly unwelcome burden. I felt as if a heavy iron helmet were weighing down on my brow and I was swaying under its weight; my thoughts were as disjointed as my footsteps as I at last went over to the other hotel to see my relatives. I sat there in a daze, amidst lively chatter, and was startled whenever I happened to look up and see their unmoved faces, which seemed to me frozen like masks by comparison with that face of his, enlivened as if by the play of light and shade as clouds cross the sky. I found the cheerful company as dreadfully inert as if I were among the dead, and while I put sugar in my cup and joined absently in the conversation, that one face kept coming before my mind's eye, as if summoned up by the surging of the blood. It had become a fervent joy to me to watch that face, and—terrible thought!—in an hour or so I would have seen it for the last time. I must involuntarily have sighed or groaned gently, for my husband's cousin leaned over to me: what was the matter, she asked, didn't I feel well? I looked so pale and sad. This unexpected question gave me a quick, easy excuse; I said I did indeed have a migraine, and perhaps she would allow me to slip away.

Thus restored to my own company, I hurried straight to my hotel. No sooner was I alone there than the sense of emptiness and abandonment came over me again, feverishly combined with a longing for the young man I was to leave today for ever. I paced up and down the room, opened shutters for no good reason, changed my dress and my ribbon, suddenly found myself in front of the looking-glass again, wondering whether, thus adorned, I might not be able to attract him after all. And I abruptly understood myself: I would do anything not to lose him! Within the space of a violent moment, my wish turned to determination. I ran down to the porter and told him I was leaving today by the night train. Now I had to hurry: I rang for the maid to help me pack—time was pressing—and as we stowed dresses and small items into my suitcases I dreamed of the coming surprise: I would accompany him to the train, and then, at the very last moment, when he was giving me his hand in farewell, I would suddenly get into the carriage with my astonished companion, I would spend that night with him, and the next night—as long as he wanted me. A kind of enchanted, wild frenzy whirled through my blood, sometimes, to the maid's surprise, I unexpectedly laughed aloud as I flung clothes into the suitcases. My senses, I felt from time to time, were all in disorder. And when the man came to take the cases down I stared at him strangely at first: it was too difficult to think of ordinary matters while I was in the grip of such inner excitement.

Time was short; it must be nearly seven, leaving me at most twenty minutes before the train left—but of course, I consoled myself, my arrival would not be a farewell now, since I had decided to accompany him on his journey as long and as far as he would have me. The hotel manservant carried the cases on ahead while I made haste to the reception desk to settle my bill. The manager was already giving me change, I was about to go on my way, when a hand gently touched my shoulder. I gave a start. It was my cousin; concerned by my apparent illness, she had come to see how I was. Everything went dark before my eyes. I did not want her here; every second I was detained meant disastrous delay, yet courtesy obliged me at least to fall into conversation with her briefly. 'You must go to bed,' she was urging me. 'I'm sure you have a temperature.' And she could well have been right, for the blood was pounding at my temples, and sometimes I felt the blue haze of approaching faintness come over my eyes. But I fended off her suggestions and took pains to seem grateful, while every word burned me, and I would have liked to thrust her ill-timed concern roughly away. However, she stayed and stayed and stayed with her unwanted solicitude, offered me eau-de-Cologne, would not be dissuaded from dabbing the cool perfume on my temples herself. Meanwhile I was counting the minutes, thinking both of him and of how to find an excuse to escape the torment of her sympathy. And the more restless I became, the more alarming did my condition seem to her; finally she was trying, almost by force, to make me go to my room and lie down. Then—in the middle of her urging—I suddenly saw the clock in the hotel lobby: it was two minutes before seven-thirty, and the train left at seven thirty-five. Brusquely, abruptly, with the brutal indifference of a desperate woman I simply stuck my hand out to my cousin—'Goodbye, I must

63

go!'—and without a moment's thought for her frozen glance, without looking round, I rushed past the surprised hotel staff and out of the door, into the street and down it to the station. From the agitated gesticulating of the hotel manservant standing waiting there with my luggage I saw, well before I got there, that time must be very short. Frantically I ran to the barrier, but there the conductor turned me back—I had forgotten to buy a ticket. And as I almost forcibly tried to persuade him to let me on the platform all the same, the train began to move. I stared at it, trembling all over, hoping at least to catch a glimpse of him at the window of one of the carriages, a wave, a greeting. But in the middle of the hurrying throng I could not see his face. The carriages rolled past faster and faster, and after a minute nothing was left before my darkened eyes but black clouds of steam.

I must have stood there as if turned to stone, for God knows how long; the hotel servant had probably spoken to me in vain several times before he ventured to touch my arm. Only then did I start and come to myself. Should he take my luggage back to the hotel, he asked. It took me a few minutes to think; no, that was impossible, after this ridiculous, frantic departure I couldn't go back there, and I never wanted to again; so I told him, impatient to be alone, to take my cases to the left luggage office. Only then, in the middle of the constantly renewed crush of people flowing clamorously into the hall and then ebbing away again, did I try to think, to think clearly, to save myself from my desperate, painful, choking sense of fury, remorse and despair, for—why not admit it?—the idea that I had missed our last meeting through my own fault was like a knife turning pitilessly within me, burning and sharp. I could have screamed aloud: that red-hot blade, penetrating ever more mercilessly, hurt so much. Perhaps only those who are strangers to passion know such sudden outbursts of emotion in their few passionate moments, moments of emotion like an avalanche or a hurricane; whole years fall from one's own breast with the fury of powers left unused. Never before or after have I felt anything like the astonishment and raging impotence of that moment when, prepared to take the boldest of steps—prepared to throw away my whole carefully conserved, collected, controlled life all at once—I suddenly found myself facing a wall of senselessness against which my passion could only beat its head helplessly.

As for what I did then, how could it be anything but equally senseless? It was foolish, even stupid, and I am almost ashamed to tell you—but I have promised myself and you to keep nothing back. I ... well, I went in search of him again. That is to say, I went in search of every moment I had spent with him. I felt irresistibly drawn to everywhere we had been together the day before, the bench in the casino grounds from which I had made him rise, the gaming hall where I had first seen him—yes, even that den of vice, just to relive the past once more, only once more. And tomorrow I would go along the Corniche in a carriage, retracing our path, so that every word and gesture would revive in my mind again—so senseless and childish was my state of confusion. But you must take into account the lightning speed with which these events overwhelmed me—I had felt little more than a single numbing blow, but now, woken too abruptly from that tumult of feeling, I wanted to go back over what I had so fleetingly experienced step by step, relishing it in retrospect by virtue of that magical self-deception we call memory. Well, some things we either do or do not understand. Perhaps you need a burning heart to comprehend them fully.

So I went first to the gaming hall to seek out the table where he had been sitting, and think of his hands among all the others there. I went in: I remembered that I had first seen him at the left-hand table in the second room. Every one of his movements was still clear before my mind's eye: I could have found his place sleepwalking, with my eyes closed and my hands outstretched.

So I went in and crossed the hall. And then ... as I looked at the crowd from the doorway ... then something strange happened. There, in the very place where I dreamed of him, there sat—ah, the hallucinations of fever! —there sat the man himself. He looked exactly as I had seen him in my daydream just now—exactly as he had been yesterday, his eyes fixed on the ball, pale as a ghost—but he it unmistakably was.

I was so shocked that I felt as if I must cry out. But I controlled my alarm at this ridiculous vision and closed my eyes. 'You're mad—dreaming—feverish,' I told myself. 'It's impossible. You're hallucinating. He left half an hour ago.' Only then did I open my eyes again. But terrible to relate, he was still sitting there exactly as he had been sitting just now, in the flesh and unmistakable. I would have known those hands among millions ... no, I wasn't dreaming, he was real. He had not left as he had promised he would, the madman was sitting there, he had taken the money I gave him for his journey and brought it here, to the green table, gambling it on his passion, oblivious of all else, while I was desperately eating my heart out for him.

I abruptly moved forward: fury blurred my vision, a frenzied, red-eyed, raging desire to take the perjurer who had so shamefully abused my confidence, my feelings, my devotion by the throat. But I controlled myself. With a deliberately slow step (and how much strength that cost me!) I went up to the table to sit directly opposite him. A gentleman courteously made way for me. Two metres of green cloth stood between us, and as if looking down from a balcony at a play on stage I could watch his face, the same face that I had seen two hours ago radiant with gratitude, illuminated by the aura of divine grace, and now entirely absorbed in the infernal fires of his passion again. The hands, those same hands that I had seen clinging to the wood of the prayer desk as he swore a most sacred oath, were now clutching at the money again like the claws of lustful vampires. For he had been winning, he must have won a very great deal: in front of him shone a jumbled pile of jettons and *louis d'ors* and banknotes, a disordered medley in which his quivering, nervous fingers were stretching and bathing with delight. I saw them pick up separate notes, stroke and fold them, I saw them turn and caress coins, then suddenly and abruptly catch up a fistful and put them down on one of the spaces. And immediately that spasmodic tic around his nostrils began again, the call of the croupier tore his greedily blazing eyes away from the money to the spinning ball, he seemed to be flowing out of himself, as it were, while his elbows might have been nailed to the green table. His total addiction was revealed as even more dreadful, more terrible than the evening before, for every move he made murdered that other image within me, the image shining as if on a golden ground that I had credulously swallowed.

So we sat there two metres away from each other; I was staring at him, but he was unaware of me. He was not looking at me or anyone else, his glance merely moved to the money, flickering unsteadily with the ball as it rolled back to rest: all his senses were contained, chasing back and forth, in that one racing green circle. To this obsessive gambler the whole world, the whole human race had shrunk to a rectangular patch of cloth. And I knew that I could stand here for hours and hours, and he would not have the faintest idea of my presence.

But I could stand it no longer. Coming to a sudden decision, I walked round the table, stepped behind him and firmly grasped his shoulder with my hand. His gaze swung upwards, for a second he stared strangely at me, glassy-eyed, like a drunk being laboriously shaken awake, eyes still vague and drowsy, clouded by inner fumes. Then he seemed to recognise me, his mouth opened, quivering, he looked happily up at me and stammered quietly, in a confused tone of mysterious confidentiality, 'It's going well ... I knew it would as soon as I came in and saw that he was here ... ' I did not understand what he meant. All I saw was that this madman was intoxicated by the game and had forgotten everything else, his promise, his appointment at the station, me and the whole world besides. But even when he was in this obsessive mood I found his ecstasy so captivating that instinctively I went along with him and asked, taken aback, who was here?

'Over there, the one-armed old Russian general,' he whispered, pressing close to me so that no one else would overhear the magic secret. 'Over there, with the white sideboards and the servant behind him. He always wins, I was watching him yesterday, he must have a system, and I always pick the same number ... He was winning yesterday too, but I made the mistake of playing on when he had left ... that was my error ... he must have won twenty thousand francs yesterday, he's winning every time now too, and I just keep following his lead. Now ... '

He broke off in mid-sentence, for the hoarse-voiced croupier was calling his '*Faites votre jeu!*' and his glance was already moving away, looking greedily at the place where the white-whiskered Russian sat, nonchalant and grave, thoughtfully putting first one gold coin and then, hesitantly, another on the fourth space. Immediately the fevered hands before me dug into the pile of money and put down a handful of coins on the same place. And when, after a minute, the croupier cried '*Zéro!*' and his rake swept the whole table bare with a single movement, he stared at the money streaming away as if at some marvel. But do you think he turned to me? No he had forgotten all about me; I had dropped out of his life, I was lost and gone from it, his whole being was intent only on the Russian general who, with complete indifference, was hefting two more gold coins in his hand, not yet sure what number to put them on.

I cannot describe my bitterness and despair. But think of my feelings: to be no more than a fly brushed carelessly aside by a man to whom one has offered one's whole life. Once again that surge of fury came over me. I seized his arm with all my strength. He started.

'You will get up at once!' I whispered to him in a soft but commanding tone. 'Remember what you swore in church today, you miserable perjurer.'

He stared at me, perplexed and pale. His eyes suddenly took on the expression of a beaten dog, his lips quivered. All at once he seemed to be remembering the past, and a horror of himself appeared to come over him.

'Yes, yes...' he stammered. 'Oh, my God, my God... yes, I'm coming, oh, forgive me...'

And his hand was already sweeping the money together, fast at first, gathering it all up with a vehement gesture, but then gradually slowing down, as if coming up against some opposing force. His eyes had fallen once more on the Russian general, who had just made his bet.

'Just a moment,' he said, quickly throwing five gold coins on the same square. 'Just this one more time... I promise you I'll come then—just this one more game... just...'

And again his voice fell silent. The ball had begun to roll and was carrying him away with it. Once again the addict had slipped away from me, from himself, flung round with the tiny ball circling in the smooth hollow of the wheel where it leaped and sprang. Once again the croupier called out the number, once again the rake carried his five coins away from him; he had lost. But he did not turn round. He had forgotten me, just like his oath in the church and the promise he had given me a minute ago. His greedy hand was moving spasmodically towards the dwindling pile of money again, and his intoxicated gaze moved only to the magnet of his will, the man opposite who brought good luck.

My patience was at an end. I shook him again, hard this time. 'Get up at once! Immediately! You said one more game...'

But then something unexpected happened. He suddenly swung round, but the face looking at me was no longer that of a humbled and confused man, it was the face of a man in a frenzy, all anger, with burning eyes and furiously trembling lips. 'Leave me alone!' he spat. 'Go away! You bring me bad luck. Whenever you're here I lose. You brought bad luck yesterday and you're bringing bad luck now. Go away!'

I momentarily froze, but now my own anger was whipped up beyond restraint by his folly.

'I am bringing you bad luck?' I snapped at him. 'You liar, you thief—you promised me ...' But I got no further, for the maniac leaped up from his seat and, indifferent to the turmoil around him, thrust me away. 'Leave me alone,' he cried, losing all control. 'I'm not under your control ... here, take your money.' And he threw me a few hundred-franc notes. 'Now leave me alone!'

He had been shouting out loud like a madman, ignoring the hundred or so people around us. They were all staring, whispering, pointing, laughing—other curious onlookers even crowded in from the hall next door. I felt as if my clothes were being torn from my body, leaving me naked before all these prying eyes. '*Silence, madame, s'il vous plaît,*' said the croupier in commanding tones, tapping his rake on the table. He meant me, the wretched creature meant me. Humiliated, overcome by shame, I stood there before the hissing, whispering curious folk like a prostitute whose customer has just thrown money at her. Two hundred, three hundred shameless eyes were turned on my face, and then—then, as I turned my gaze evasively aside, overwhelmed by this filthy deluge of humiliation and shame, my own eyes met two others, piercing and astonished—it was my cousin looking at me appalled, her mouth open, one hand raised as if in horror.

That struck home; before she could stir or recover from her surprise I stormed out of the hall. I got as far as the bench outside, the same bench on which the gambling addict had collapsed yesterday. I dropped to the hard, pitiless wood, as powerless, exhausted and shattered as he had been.

All that is twenty-four years ago, yet when I remember the moment when I stood there before a thousand strangers, lashed by their scorn, the blood freezes in my veins. And once again I feel, in horror, how weak, poor and flabby a substance whatever we call by the names of soul, spirit or feeling must be after all, not to mention what we describe as pain, since all this, even to the utmost degree, is insufficient to destroy the suffering flesh of the tormented body entirely—for we do survive such hours and our blood continues to pulse, instead of dying and falling like a tree struck by lightning. Only for a sudden moment, for an instant, did this pain tear through my joints so hard that I dropped on the bench breathless and dazed, with a positively voluptuous premonition that I must die. But as I was saying, pain is cowardly, it gives way before the overpowering will to live which seems to cling more strongly to our flesh than all the mortal suffering of the spirit. Even to myself, I cannot explain my feelings after such a shattering blow, but I did rise to my feet, although I did not know what to do. Suddenly it occurred to me that my suitcases were already at the station, and I thought suddenly that I must get away, away from here, away from this accursed, this infernal building. Taking no notice of anyone, I made haste to the station and asked when the next train for Paris left. At ten o'clock, the porter told me, and I immediately retrieved my luggage. Ten o'clock—so exactly twenty-four hours had passed since that terrible meeting, twenty-four hours so full of changeable, contradictory feelings that my inner world was shattered for ever. At first, however, I felt nothing but that one word in the constantly hammering, pounding rhythm: away, away, away! The pulses behind my brow kept driving it into my temples like a wedge: away, away, away! Away from this town, away from myself, home to my own people, to my own old life! I travelled through the night to Paris, changed from one station to another and travelled direct to Boulogne, from Boulogne to Dover, from Dover to London, from London to my son's house—all in one headlong flight, without stopping to think or consider, forty-eight hours without sleep, without speaking to anyone, without eating, forty-eight hours during which the wheels of all the trains rattled out that one word: away, away, away! When at last I arrived unexpectedly at my son's country house, everyone was alarmed; there must have been something in my bearing and my eyes that gave me away. My son came to embrace and kiss me, but I shrank away: I could not bear the thought of his touching lips that I felt were disgraced. I avoided all questions, asked only for a bath, because I needed to wash not only the dirt of the journey from my body but all of the passion of that obsessed, unworthy man that seemed to cling to it. Then I dragged myself up to my room and slept a benumbed and stony sleep for twelve or fourteen hours, a sleep such as I have never slept before or since, and after it I know what it must be like to lie dead in a coffin. My family cared for me as for a sick woman, but their affection only hurt me, I was ashamed of their respect, and had to keep preventing myself from suddenly screaming out loud how I had betrayed, forgotten and abandoned them all for the sake of a foolish, crazy passion.

Then, aimless again, I went back to France and a little town where I knew no one, for I was pursued by the delusion that at the very first glance everyone could see my shame and my changed nature from the outside, I felt so betrayed, so soiled to the depths of my soul. Sometimes, when I woke in my bed in the morning, I felt a dreadful fear of opening my eyes. Once again I would be overcome by the memory of that night when I suddenly woke beside a half-naked stranger, and then, as I had before, all I wanted was to die immediately.

But after all, time is strong, and age has the curious power of devaluing all our feelings. You feel death coming closer, its shadow falls black across your path, and things seem less brightly coloured, they do not go to the heart so much, they lose much of their dangerous violence. Gradually I recovered from the shock, and when, many years later, I met a young Pole who was an attaché of the Austrian Embassy at a party, and in answer to my inquiry about that family he told me that one of his cousin's sons had shot himself ten years before in Monte Carlo, I did not even tremble. It hardly hurt any more; perhaps—why deny one's egotism?—I was even glad of it, for now my last fear of ever meeting him again was gone. I had no witness against me left but my own memory. Since then I have become calmer. Growing old, after all, means that one no longer fears the past.

And now you will understand why I suddenly brought myself to tell you about my own experience. When you defended Madame Henriette and said, so passionately, that twenty-four hours could determine a woman's whole life, I felt that you meant me; I was grateful to you, since for the first time I felt myself, as it were, confirmed in my existence. And then I thought it would be good to unburden myself of it all for once, and perhaps then the spell on me would be broken, the eternal looking back; perhaps I can go to Monte Carlo tomorrow and enter the same hall where I met my fate without feeling hatred for him or myself. Then the stone will roll off my soul, laying its full weight over the past and preventing it from ever rising again. It has done me good to tell you all this. I feel easier in my mind now and almost light at heart ... thank you for that."

With these words she had suddenly risen, and I felt that she had reached the end. Rather awkwardly, I sought for something to say. But she must have felt my emotion, and quickly waved it away.

"No, please, don't speak ... I'd rather you didn't reply or say anything to me. Accept my thanks for listening, and I wish you a good journey."

She stood opposite me, holding out her hand in farewell. Instinctively I looked at her face, and the countenance of this old woman who stood before me with a kindly yet slightly ashamed expression seemed to me wonderfully touching. Whether it was the reflection of past passion or mere confusion that suddenly dyed her cheeks with red, the colour rising to her white hair, she stood there just like a girl, in a bridal confusion of memories and ashamed of her own confession. Involuntarily moved, I very much wanted to say something to express my respect for her, but my throat was too constricted. So I leaned down and respectfully kissed the faded hand that trembled slightly like an autumn leaf.

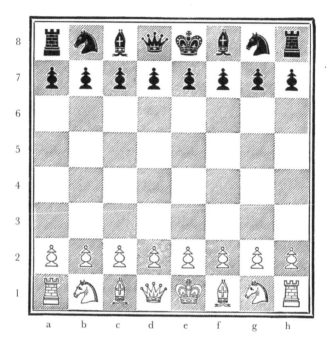

THE ROYAL GAME

Translated from the German by BW Huebsch

THE BIG LINER, due to sail from New York to Buenos Aires at midnight, was filled with the activity and bustle incident to the last hour. Visitors who had come to see their friends scurried hither and thither, pageboys with caps smartly cocked slithered through the public rooms shouting names snappily, baggage, parcels and flowers were being hauled about, inquisitive children ran up and down companion-ways, while the deck orchestra provided persistent accompaniment. I stood talking to an acquaintance on the promenade deck, somewhat apart from the hubbub, when two or three flash-bulbs sprayed sharply near us, evidently for press photos of some prominent passenger at a last-minute interview. My friend looked in that direction and smiled.

"You have a queer bird on board, that Czentovic."

And as my face must have revealed that the statement meant nothing to me he added, by way of explanation, "Mirko Czentovic, the world chess champion. He has just finished off America in a coast-to-coast exhibition tour and is on his way to capture Argentina."

This served to recall not only the name of the young world champion but also a few details relating to his rocket-like career; my friend, a more observant newspaper reader than I, was able to eke them out with a string of anecdotes. At a single stroke, about a year ago, Czentovic had aligned himself with the most celebrated elder statesmen of the art of chess, such as Alekhin, Capablanca, Tartakover, Lasker, Boguljobov; not since the appearance of the nine-year-old prodigy, Reshevsky, in New York in 1922, had a newcomer crashed into that famed guild to the accompaniment of such widespread interest. It seems that Czentovic's intellectual equipment, at the beginning, gave small promise of so brilliant a career. The secret soon seeped through that in his private capacity this champion wasn't able to write a single sentence in any language without misspelling a word, and that, as one of his vexed colleagues, wrathfully sarcastic, put it, "He enjoys equal ignorance in every field of culture". His father, a poverty-stricken Yugoslavian boatman on the Danube, had been run down in his tiny vessel one night by a grain steamer, and the orphaned boy, then twelve, was taken in charge, out of pity, by the pastor of their obscure village. The good man did his level best to instil into the indolent, slow-speaking, low-browed child at home what he seemed unable to grasp in the village school.

But all his efforts proved in vain. Mirko stared blankly at the writing exercise just as if the strokes had not already been explained a hundred times; his lumbering brain lacked the power to grasp even the simplest subjects. At fourteen he still counted with his fingers, and it was only by dint of great strain that he could read a book or newspaper. Yet none could say that Mirko was unwilling or disobedient. Whatever he was told to do he did: fetched water, split wood, worked in the field, washed up the kitchen, and he could be relied upon to execute—even if with exasperating slowness—every service that was demanded. But what grieved the kindly pastor most about the blockhead was his total lack of co-operation. He performed no deed unless specially directed, asked no questions, never played with other lads, and sought no occupation of his own accord; after Mirko had concluded his work about the house, he would sit idly with that empty stare one sees with grazing sheep, without participating in the slightest in what might be going on. Of an evening, while the pastor sucked at his long peasant pipe and played his customary three games of chess with the police-sergeant, the fair-haired dull-wit squatted silently alongside them, staring from under his heavy lids, seemingly sleepy and indifferent, at the chequered board.

One winter evening, while the two men were absorbed in their daily game, a rapid crescendo of bells gave notice of a quickly approaching sleigh. A peasant, his cap covered with snow, stamped in hastily to tell the pastor that his mother lay dying and to ask his immediate attendance in the hope that there was still time to administer extreme unction. The priest accompanied him at once. The police-sergeant, who had not yet finished his beer, lit a fresh pipe preparatory to leaving, and was about to draw on his heavy sheepskin boots when he noticed how immovably Mirko's gaze was fastened on the board with its interrupted game.

"Well, do you want to finish it?" he said jocularly, fully convinced that the sleepyhead had no notion of how to move a single piece. The boy looked up shyly, nodded assent, and took the pastor's place. After fourteen moves the sergeant was beaten and he had to concede that his defeat was in no way attributable to avoidable carelessness. The second game had the same result.

"Balaam's ass!" cried the astounded pastor upon his return, explaining to the policeman, a lesser expert in the Bible, that two thousand years ago there had been a similar miracle of a dumb person suddenly endowed with the speech of wisdom. The late hour notwithstanding, the good man could not forgo challenging his half-illiterate helper to a contest. Mirko beat him too, with ease. He played toughly, slowly, deliberately, never once raising his bowed, broad brow from the chessboard. But he played with irrefutable certainty, and in the days that followed neither the priest nor the policeman was able to win a single game.

The priest, best able to assess his ward's various shortcomings, now became curious as to the manner in which this one-sided singular gift would resist a severer test. After Mirko had been made somewhat presentable by the efforts of the village barber, the priest drove him in his sleigh to the nearby town where he knew that many chess-players—a cut above him in ability, he was aware from experience—were always to be found in the café on the main square. The pastor's entrance, as he steered the straw-haired, red-cheeked fifteen-year-old before him, created no small stir in the circle; the boy, in his sheepskin jacket (woollen side in) and high boots, eyes shyly downcast, stood aside until summoned to a chess-table.

Mirko lost the first encounter because his master had never employed the Sicilian defence. The next game, with the best player of the lot, resulted in a draw. But in the third game and the fourth and all that came after he slew them, one after the other.

It so happens that little provincial towns of Yugoslavia are seldom the theatre of exciting events; consequently, this first appearance of the peasant champion before the assembled worthies became no less than a sensation. It was unanimously decided to keep the boy in town until the next day for a special gathering of the chess club and, in particular, for the benefit of Count Simczic of the castle, a chess fanatic. The priest, who now regarded his ward with quite a new pride, but whose joy of discovery was subordinate to the sense of duty which called him home to his Sunday service, consented to leave him for further tests. The chess group put young Czentovic up at the local hotel, where he saw a water-closet for the first time in his life.

The chess-room was crowded to capacity on Sunday afternoon. Mirko faced the board immobile for four hours, spoke not a word, and never looked up; one player after another fell before him. Finally a multiple game was proposed; it took a while before they could make clear to the novice that he had to play against several contestants at one and the same time. No sooner had Mirko grasped the procedure than he adapted himself to it, and trod slowly with heavy, creaking shoes from table to table, eventually winning seven of the eight games.

Grave consultations now took place. True, strictly speaking, the new champion was not of the town, yet the innate national pride had received a lively fillip. Here was a chance, at last, for this town, so small that its existence was hardly suspected, to put itself on the map by sending a great man into the world. A vaudeville agent named Koller, who supplied the local garrison cabaret with talent, offered to obtain professional training for the youth from a Viennese expert whom he knew, and to see him through for a year if the deficit were made good. Count Simczic, who in his sixty years of daily chess had never encountered so remarkable an opponent, signed the guarantee promptly. That day marked the opening of the astonishing career of the Danube boatman's son.

It took only six months for Mirko to master every secret of chess technique, though with one odd limitation which later became apparent to the experts of the game and caused many a sneer. He was never able to memorise a single game or, to use the professional term, to play blind. He lacked completely the ability to conceive the board in the limitless space of the imagination. He had to have the field of sixty-four black and white squares and the thirty-two pieces tangibly before him; even when he had attained international fame he carried a folding pocket board with him in order to be able to reconstruct a game or work on a problem by visual means. This defect, in itself not important, betrayed a want of imaginative power and provoked animated discussions among chess enthusiasts similar to those in musical circles when it discovers that an outstanding virtuoso or conductor is unable to play or direct without a score. This singularity, however, was no obstacle to Mirko's stupendous rise. At seventeen he already possessed a dozen prizes, at eighteen he won the Hungarian Masters, and finally, at twenty, the championship of the world. The boldest experts, every one of them immeasurably his superior in brains, imagination, and audacity, fell before his tough, cold logic as did Napoleon before the clumsy Kutusov and Hannibal before Fabius Cunctator, of whom Livy records that his traits of phlegm and imbecility were already conspicuous in his childhood. Thus it occurred that the illustrious gallery of chess masters, which included eminent representatives of widely varied intellectual fields—philosophers, mathematicians, constructive, imaginative, and often creative talents —was invaded by a complete outsider, a heavy, taciturn peasant from whom not even the most cunning journalists were ever able to extract a word that would help to make a story. Yet, however he may have deprived the newspapers of polished phrases, substitutes in the way of anecdotes about his person were numerous, for, inescapably, the moment he arose from the board at which he was the incomparable master, Czentovic became a grotesque, an almost comic figure. In spite of his correct dress, his fashionable cravat with its too ostentatious pearl tiepin, and his carefully manicured nails, he remained in manners and behaviour the narrow-minded lout who was accustomed to sweeping out the priest's kitchen. He utilised his gift and his fame to squeeze out all the money they would yield, displaying petty and often vulgar greed, always with a shameless clumsiness that aroused his professional colleagues' ridicule and anger. He travelled from town to town, stopped at the cheapest hotels, played for any club that would pay his fee, sold the advertising rights in his portrait to a soap manufacturer, and, oblivious of his competitors' scorn—they being aware that he hardly knew how to write—attached his name to a *Philosophy of Chess* that had been written by a hungry Galician student for a business-minded publisher. As with all leathery dispositions, he was wanting in any appreciation of the ludicrous; from the time he became champion he regarded himself as the most important man in the world, and the consciousness of having beaten all those clever, intellectual, brilliant speakers and writers in their own field and of earning more than they, transformed his early unsureness into a cold and awkwardly flaunted pride.

"And how can one expect that such rapid fame should fail to befuddle so empty a head?" concluded my friend who had just advanced those classic examples of Czentovic's childish lust for rank. "Why shouldn't a twenty-one-year-old lad from the Banat be afflicted with a frenzy of vanity if, suddenly, by merely shoving figures around on a wooden board, he can earn more in a week than his whole village does in a year by chopping down trees under the bitterest conditions? Besides, isn't it damned easy to take yourself for a great man if you're not burdened with the slightest suspicion that a Rembrandt, a Beethoven, a Dante, a Napoleon, ever even existed? There's just one thing in that immured brain of his—the knowledge that he hasn't lost a game of chess for months, and as he happens not to dream that the world holds other values than chess and money, he has every reason to be infatuated with himself."

The information communicated by my friend could not fail to excite my special curiosity. I have always been fascinated by all types of monomania, by persons wrapped up in a single idea; for the stricter the limits a man sets for himself, the more clearly he approaches the eternal. Just such seemingly world-aloof persons create their own remarkable and quite unique miniature worlds, and work, termite-like, in their particular medium. Thus I made no bones about my intention to examine this specimen of one-track intellect under a magnifying glass during the twelve-day journey to Rio.

"You'll be out of luck," my friend warned me. "So far as I know, nobody has succeeded in extracting the least bit of psychological material from Czentovic. Underneath all his abysmal limitations this sly farmhand conceals the wisdom not to expose himself. The procedure is simple: except with such compatriots of his own circle as he contrives to meet in ordinary taverns he avoids all conversation. When he senses a person of culture he retreats into his shell; that's why nobody can flatter himself on having heard him say something stupid or on having sounded the presumably bottomless depths of his ignorance."

As a matter of fact, my friend was right. It proved utterly impossible to approach Czentovic during the first few days of the voyage, unless by intruding rudely, which, of course, isn't my way. He did sometimes appear on the promenade deck, but then always with hands clasped behind his back in a posture of dignified self-absorption, like Napoleon in the familiar painting; and, at that, those peripatetic exhibitions were carried off in such haste and so jerkily that to gain one's end one would have had to trot after him. The lounges, the bar, the smoking-room, saw nothing of him. A steward of whom I made confidential inquiries revealed that he spent the greater part of the day in his cabin with a large chess-board on which he replayed games or worked out new problems.

After three days it angered me to think that his defence tactics were more effective than my will to approach him. I had never before had a chance to know a great chess-player personally, and the more I now sought to familiarise myself with the type, the more incomprehensible seemed a lifelong brain activity that rotated exclusively about a space composed of sixty-four black and white squares. I was well aware from my own experience of the mysterious attraction of the "royal game", which among all games contrived by man rises superior to the tyranny of chance and bestows its palm only on mental attainment, or rather on a definite form of mental endowment. But is it not an offensively narrow construction to call chess a game? Is it not a science, a technique, an art, that sways among these categories as Mohammed's coffin does between heaven and earth, at once a union of all contradictory concepts: primaeval yet ever new; mechanical in operation yet effective only through the imagination; bounded in geometric space though boundless in its combinations; ever-developing yet sterile; thought that leads to nothing; mathematics that produce no result; art without works; architecture without substance, and nevertheless, as proved by evidence, more lasting in its being and presence than all books and achievements; the only game that belongs to all peoples and all ages; of which none knows the divinity that bestowed it on the world, to slay boredom, to sharpen the senses, to exhilarate the spirit. One searches for its beginning and for its end. Children can learn its simple rules, duffers succumb to its temptation, yet within this immutable tight square it creates a particular species of master not to be compared with any other—persons destined for chess alone, specific geniuses in whom vision, patience, and technique are operative through a distribution no less precisely ordained than in mathematicians, poets, composers, but merely united on a different level. In the heyday of physiognomical research a Gall would perhaps have dissected the brains of such masters of chess to establish whether a particular coil in the grey matter of the brain, a sort of chess muscle or chess bump, was more conspicuously developed than in other skulls. How a physiognomist would have been fascinated by the case of a Czentovic where that which is genius appears interspersed with an absolute inertia of the intellect, like a single vein of gold in a ton of dead rock! It stands to reason that so unusual a game, one touched with genius, must create out of itself fitting matadors. This I always knew, but what was difficult and almost impossible to conceive, was the life of a mentally alert person whose world contracts to a narrow, black-and-white one-way street; who seeks ultimate triumphs in the to-and-fro, forward-and-backward movement of thirty-two pieces; a being who, by a new opening in which the knight is preferred to the pawn, apprehends greatness and the immortality that goes with casual mention in a chess handbook—of a man of spirit who, escaping madness, can unremittingly devote all of his mental energy during ten, twenty, thirty, forty years to the ludicrous effort to corner a wooden king on a wooden board!

And here, for the first time, one of these phenomena, one of these singular geniuses (or should I say puzzling fools?) was close to me, six cabins away, and I, unfortunate, for whom curiosity about mental problems manifested itself in a kind of passion, seemed unable to effect my purpose. I conjured up the absurdest ruses: should I tickle his vanity by the offer of an interview in an important paper, or engage his greed by proposing a lucrative exhibition tour of Scotland? Finally it occurred to me that the hunter's never-failing practice is to lure the woodcock by imitating its mating cry, so what more successful way was there of attracting a chess master's attention to myself than by playing chess?

At no time had I ever permitted chess to absorb me seriously, for the simple reason that it meant nothing to me but a pastime; if I spend an hour at the board it is not because I want to subject myself to a strain but, on the contrary, to relieve mental tension. I 'play' at chess in the literal sense of the word, whereas to real devotees it is serious business. Chess, like love, cannot be played alone, and up to that time I had no idea whether there were other chess lovers on board. In order to attract them from their lairs I set a primitive trap in the smoking-room in that my wife (whose game is even weaker than mine) and I sat at a chessboard as a decoy. Sure enough, we had made no more than six moves before one passer-by stopped, another asked permission to watch, and before long the desired partner materialised. McConnor was his name; a Scottish foundation-engineer who, I learned, had made a large fortune drilling for oil in California. He was a robust specimen with an almost square jaw and strong teeth, and a rich complexion pronouncedly rubicund as a result, at least in part surely, of copious indulgence in whisky. His conspicuously broad, almost vehemently athletic shoulders made themselves unpleasantly noticeable in his game, for this Mr McConnor typified those self-important worshippers of success who regard defeat in even a harmless contest as a blow to their self-esteem. Accustomed to achieving his ends ruthlessly, and spoiled by material success, this massive self-made man was so thoroughly saturated with his sense of superiority that opposition of any kind became undue resistance if not insult. After losing the first round he sulked and began to explain in detail, and dictatorially, that it would not have happened but for a momentary oversight; in the third he ascribed his failure to the noise in the adjoining room; never would he lose a game without at once demanding revenge. This ambitious crabbedness amused me at first, but as time went on I accepted it as the unavoidable accompaniment to my real purpose—to tempt the master to our table.

By the third day it worked—but only half-way. It may be that Czentovic observed us at the chess-board through a window from the promenade deck or that he just happened to be honouring the smoking-room with his presence; anyway, as soon as he perceived us interlopers toying with the tools of his trade, he involuntarily stepped a little nearer and, keeping a deliberate distance, cast a searching glance at our board. It was McConnor's move. This one move was sufficient to apprise Czentovic how little a further pursuit of our dilettantish striving was worthy of his expert interest. With the same matter-of-course gesture with which one of us disposes of a poor detective story that has been proffered in a library—without even thumbing its pages—he turned away from our table and left the room. "Weighed in the balance and found wanting," I thought, slightly stung by the cool, contemptuous look, and to give vent to my ill humour in some fashion, I said to McConnor, "Your move didn't seem to impress the master."

"Which master?"

I told him that the man who had just walked by after glancing disapprovingly at our game was Czentovic, international chess champion. I added that we would be able to survive without taking his contempt too greatly to heart; the poor have to cook with water. But to my astonishment these idle words of mine produced quite an unexpected result. Immediately he became excited, he forgot our game, and his ambition took on an almost audible throbbing. He had no notion that Czentovic was on board: Czentovic simply had to give him a game; the only time he had ever played with a champion was in a multiple game when he was one of forty; even that was fearfully exciting, and he had come quite near winning. Did I know the champion personally?—I didn't. Would I not invite him to join us?—I declined on the ground that I was aware of Czentovic's reluctance to make new acquaintances. Besides, what charm would taking on third-rate players hold for a champion?

It would have been just as well not to say that about third-rate players to a man of McConnor's brand of conceit. Annoyed, he leaned back and declared gruffly that, as for himself, he couldn't believe that Czentovic would decline a gentleman's courteous challenge; he'd see to that. Upon getting a brief description of the master's person he stormed out, indifferent to our unfinished game, uncontrollably impatient to intercept Czentovic on the deck. Again I sensed that there was no holding the possessor of such broad shoulders once his will was involved in an undertaking.

I waited, somewhat tensed. Some ten minutes elapsed and McConnor returned, not in too good humour, it seemed to me.

"Well?" I asked.

"You were right," he answered, a bit annoyed. "Not a very pleasant gentleman. I introduced myself and told him who I am. He didn't even put out his hand. I tried to make him understand that all of us on board would be proud and honoured if he'd play the lot of us. But he was cursed stiff-necked about it; said he was sorry but his contract obligations to his agent definitely precluded any game during his entire tour except for a fee. And his minimum is two hundred and fifty dollars per game."

I had to laugh. The thought would never have come to me that one could make so much money by pushing figures from black squares to white ones. "Well, I hope you took leave of him with courtesy equal to his."

McConnor, however, remained perfectly serious. "The match is to come off at three tomorrow afternoon. Here in the smoking-room. I hope he won't make mincemeat of us easily."

"What! You promised him the two hundred and fifty dollars?" I cried, quite taken aback.

"Why not? It's his business. If I had a toothache and there happened to be a dentist aboard, I wouldn't expect him to extract my tooth for nothing. The man's right to ask a fat price; in every line the big shots are the best traders. So far as I'm concerned, the less complicated the business, the better. I'd rather pay in cash than have your Mr Czentovic do me a favour and in the end have to say 'thank you.' Anyway, many an evening at the club has cost me more than two hundred and fifty dollars without giving me a chance to play a world champion. It's no disgrace for a third-rate player to be beaten by a Czentovic."

It amused me to note how deeply I had injured McConnor's self-love with that 'third-rate'. But as he was disposed to foot the bill it was not for me to remark on his wounded ambition which promised at last to afford me an acquaintance with my odd fish. Promptly we notified the four or five others who had revealed themselves as chess-players of the approaching event and reserved not only our own table but the adjacent ones so that we might suffer the least possible disturbance from passengers strolling by.

Next day all our group was assembled at the appointed hour. The centre seat opposite that of the master was allotted to McConnor as a matter of course; his nervousness found outlet in the smoking of strong cigars, one after another, and in restlessly glancing repeatedly at the clock. The champion let us wait a good ten minutes—my friend's tale prompted the surmise that something like this would happen—thus height-ening the impressiveness of his entry. He approached the table calmly and imperturbably. He offered no greeting. "You know who I am and I'm not interested in who you are" was what his discourtesy seemed to imply, but he began in a dry, businesslike way to lay down the conditions. Since there were not enough boards on the ship for separate games he proposed that we should play against him collectively. After each of his moves he would retire to the end of the room so that his presence might not affect our consultations. As soon as our countermove had been made we were to strike a glass with a spoon, no table-bell being available. He proposed, if it pleased us, ten minutes as the maximum time for each move. Like timid pupils we accepted every suggestion unquestioningly. Czentovic drew black at the choice of colours; while still standing he made the first counter-move, then turned at once to go to the designated waiting-place, where he reclined lazily while carelessly examining an illustrated magazine.

There is little point in reporting the game. It ended, as it could not but end, in our complete defeat, and by the twenty-fourth move at that. There was nothing particularly astonish-ing about an international champion wiping off half a dozen mediocre or sub-mediocre players with his left hand; what did disgust us, though, was the lordly manner with which Czentovic caused us to feel, all too plainly, that it was with his left hand that we had been disposed of. Each time he would give a quick, seemingly careless look at the board, and would look indolently past us as if we ourselves were dead wooden figures; and this impertinent proceeding reminded one irresistibly of the way one throws a mangy dog a morsel without taking the trouble to look at him. According to my way of thinking, if he had any sensitivity he might have shown us our mistakes or cheered us up with a friendly word. Even at the conclusion this sub-human chess automaton uttered no syllable, but, after

saying "check-mate," stood motionless at the table waiting to
ascertain whether another game was desired. I had already
risen with the thought of indicating by a gesture—helpless as
one always remains in the face of thick-skinned rudeness—that
as far as I was concerned the pleasure of our acquaintance
was ended now that the dollars-and-cents part of it was over,
when, to my anger, McConnor, next to me, spoke up hoarsely:
"*Revanche!*"

The note of challenge startled me; McConnor at this moment
seemed much more like a pugilist about to put up his fists than
a polite gentleman. Whether it was Czentovic's disagreeable
treatment of us that affected him or merely McConnor's own
pathological irritable ambition, suffice it that the latter had
undergone a complete change. Red in the face up to his hair,
his nostrils taut, he breathed hard and a sharp fold separated
the bitten lips from his belligerently projected jaw. I recognised
with disquiet that flicker of the eyes that indicates uncontrollable passion, such as seizes players at roulette when the right colour fails to come after the sixth or seventh successively-doubled
stake. Instantly I knew that this fanatical climber would, even
at the cost of his entire fortune, play against Czentovic and play
and play and play, for simple or doubled stakes, until he won at
least a single game. If Czentovic stuck to it, McConnor would
prove a gold-mine that would yield him a nice few thousands
by the time Buenos Aires came in sight.

Czentovic remained unmoved. "If you please," he responded
politely. "You gentlemen will take black this time."

There was nothing different about the second game except
that our group became larger because of a few added onlookers, and livelier, too. McConnor stared fixedly at the board
as if he willed to magnetise the chess-men to victory; I sensed
that he would have paid a thousand dollars with delight if he
could but shout "check-mate" at our cold-snouted adversary.
Oddly enough, something of his sullen excitement entered

unconsciously into all of us. Every single move was discussed with greater emotion than before; always we would wrangle up to the last moment before agreeing to signal Czentovic to return to the table. We had come to the seventeenth move and, to our own surprise, entered on a combination which seemed staggeringly advantageous because we had been enabled to advance a pawn to the last square but one; we needed but to move it forward to **c1** to win a second queen. Not that we felt too comfortable about so obvious an opportunity; we were united in suspecting that the advantage which we seemed to have wrested could be no more than bait dangled by Czentovic, whose vision enabled him to view the situation from a distance of several moves. Yet in spite of common examination and discussion, we were unable to explain it as a feint. At last, at the limit of our ten minutes, we decided to risk the move. McConnor's fingers were on the pawn to move it to the last square when he felt his arm gripped and heard a voice, low and impetuous, whisper, "For God's sake! Don't!"

Involuntarily we all turned about. I recognised in the man of some forty-five years, who must have joined the group during the last few minutes in which we were absorbed in the problem before us, one whose narrow sharp face had already arrested my attention on deck strolls because of its extraordinary, almost chalky pallor. Conscious of our gaze, he continued rapidly:

"If you make a queen he will immediately attack with the bishop, then you'll take it with your knight. Meantime, however, he moves his pawn to **d7**, threatens your rook, and even if you check with the knight you're lost and will be wiped out in nine or ten moves. It's practically the constellation that Alekhin introduced when he played Boguljobov in 1922 at the championship tournament at Pistany."

Astonished, McConnor released the pawn and, like the rest of us, stared in amazement at the man who had descended in our midst like a rescuing angel. Anyone who can reckon a mate nine moves ahead must necessarily be a first-class expert, perhaps even a contestant now on his way to the tournament to seize the championship, so that his sudden presence, his thrust into the game at precisely the critical moment, verged almost on the supernatural.

McConnor was the first to compose himself. "What do you advise?" he asked tensely.

"Don't advance yet; rather a policy of evasion. First of all, get the king out of the danger line from **g8** to **h7**. Then he'll probably transfer his attack to the other flank. Then you parry that with the rook, **c8-c4**; two moves and he will have lost not only a pawn but his superiority, and if you maintain your defensive properly you may be able to make it a draw. That's the best you can get out of it."

We gasped, amazed. The precision no less than the rapidity of his calculations dizzied us; it was as if he had been reading the moves from a printed page. For all that, this unsuspected turn by which, thanks to his cutting in, the contest with a world champion promised a draw, worked wonders. Animated by a single thought, we moved aside so as not to obstruct his observation of the board.

Again McConnor inquired: "The king, from **g8** to **h7**?"

"Surely. The main thing is to duck."

McConnor obeyed and we rapped on the glass. Czentovic came forward at his habitual even pace, his eyes swept the board and took in the countermove. Then he moved the pawn **h2-h4** on the king's flank exactly as our unknown aid had predicted. Already the latter was whispering excitedly:

"The rook forward, the rook, from **c8** to **c4**; then he'll first have to cover the pawn. That won't help him, though. Don't bother about his pawns but attack with the knight **c3-d5**, and the balance is again restored. Press the offensive instead of defending."

We had no idea of what he meant. He might just as well have been talking Chinese. But once under his spell McConnor did as he had been bidden. Again we struck the glass to recall Czentovic. This was the first time that he made no quick decision; instead he looked fixedly at the board. His eyebrows contracted involuntarily. Then he made his move, the one which our stranger had said he would, and turned to go. Yet before he started off something novel and unexpected happened. Czentovic raised his eyes and surveyed our ranks; plainly he wanted to ascertain who it was that offered such unaccustomed energetic resistance.

From this moment our excitement grew immeasurably. Thus far we had played without genuine hope, but now every pulse beat hotly at the thought of breaking Czentovic's cold disdain. Without loss of time our new friend had directed the next move and we were ready to call Czentovic back. My fingers trembled as I hit the spoon against the glass. And now we registered our first triumph. Czentovic, who hitherto had executed his purpose standing, hesitated, hesitated and finally sat down. He did this slowly and heavily, but that was enough to cancel—in a physical sense if in no other—the difference in levels that had existed between us. We had necessitated his acknowledgement of equality, spatially at least. He cogitated long, his eyes resting immovably on the board so that one could scarcely discern the pupils under the heavy lids, and under the strained application his mouth opened gradually, which gave him a rather foolish look. Czentovic reflected for some minutes, then made a move and rose. At once our friend said half-audibly:

"A stall! Well thought out! But don't yield to it! Force an exchange, he's got to exchange, then we'll get a draw and not even the gods can help him."

McConnor did as he was told. The succeeding manoeuvres between the two men—we others had long since become mere extras—consisted of a back-and-forth that we were unable to comprehend. After some seven moves Czentovic looked up after a period of silence and said, "Draw."

For a moment a total stillness reigned. Suddenly one heard the rushing of the waves and the jazzing radio in the adjacent drawing-room; one picked out every step on the promenade outside and the faint thin murmuring of the wind that carried through the window-frames. None of us breathed; it had come upon us too abruptly and we were nothing less than frightened in the face of the impossible: that this stranger should have been able to force his will on the world champion in a contest already half-lost. McConnor shoved himself back and relaxed, and his suppressed breathing became audible in the joyous "Ah" that passed his lips. I took another look at Czentovic. It had already seemed to me during the later moves that he grew paler. But he understood how to maintain his poise. He persisted in his apparent imperturbability and asked, in a negligent tone, as he pushed the figures off the board with a steady hand "Would you like to have a third game, gentlemen?"

The question was matter-of-fact, just business. What was noteworthy was that he ignored McConnor and looked straight and intently into the eyes of our rescuer. Just as a horse takes a new rider's measure by the firmness of his seat, he must have become aware of who was his real, in fact his only, opponent. We could not help but follow his gaze and look eagerly at the unknown. However before he could collect himself and formulate an answer, McConnor, in his eager excitement, had already cried to him in triumph:

"Certainly, no doubt about it! But this time you've got to play him alone! You against Czentovic!"

What followed was quite extraordinary. The stranger, who curiously enough was still staring with a strained expression at the bare board, became nervous upon hearing the lusty call and perceiving that he was the centre of observation. He looked confused.

"By no means, gentlemen," he said haltingly, clearly perplexed. "Quite out of the question. You'll have to leave me
out. It's twenty, no, twenty-five years since I sat at a chess-board
and ... and I'm only now conscious of my bad manners in crash-
ing into your game without so much as a by-your-leave ... Please
excuse my presumption. I don't want to interfere further." And
before we could recover from our astonishment he had left us
and gone out.

"But that's just impossible!" boomed the irascible McConnor,
pounding with his fist. "Out of the question that this fellow
hasn't played chess for twenty-five years. Why, he calculated
every move, every countermove, five or six in advance. You can't
shake that out of your sleeve. Just out of the question—isn't
it?"

Involuntarily, McConnor turned to Czentovic with the last
question. But the champion preserved his unalterable frigidity.

"It's not for me to express an opinion. In any case there
was something strange and interesting about the man's game;
that's why I purposely left him a chance."

With that he rose lazily and added, in his objective manner:
"If he or you gentlemen should want another game tomorrow,
I'm at your disposal from three o'clock on."

We were unable to suppress our chuckles. Every one of us
knew that the chance which Czentovic had allowed his nameless antagonist had not been prompted by generosity and that
the remark was no more than a childish ruse to cover his frus-
tration. It served to stimulate the more actively our desire to
witness the utter humbling of so unshakeable an arrogance.
All at once we peaceable, indolent passengers were seized by a
mad, ambitious will to battle, for the thought that just on our
ship, in mid-ocean, the palm might be wrested from the champion—a record that would be flashed to every news agency in
the world—fascinated us challengingly. Added to that was the
lure of the mysterious which emanated from the unexpected

entry of our saviour at the crucial instant, and the contrast between his almost painful modesty and the rigid self-consciousness of the professional. Who was this unknown? Had destiny utilised this opportunity to command the revelation of a yet undiscovered chess phenomenon? Or was it that we were dealing with an expert who, for some undisclosed reason, craved anonymity? We discussed these various possibilities excitedly; the most extreme hypotheses were not sufficiently extreme to reconcile the stranger's puzzling shyness with his surprising declaration in the face of his demonstrated mastery. On one point, however, we were of one mind: to forgo no chance of a renewal of the contest. We resolved to exert ourselves to the limit to induce our godsend to play Czentovic the next day, McConnor pledging himself to foot the bill. Having in the meantime learned from the steward that the unknown was an Austrian, I, as his compatriot, was delegated to present our request.

Soon I found our man reclining in his deck-chair, reading. In the moment of approach I used the opportunity to observe him. The sharply chiselled head rested on the cushion in a posture of slight exhaustion; again I was struck by the extraordinary colourlessness of the comparatively youthful face framed at the temples by glistening white hair, and I got the impression, I cannot say why, that this person must have aged suddenly. No sooner did I stand before him than he rose courteously and introduced himself by a name that was familiar to me as belonging to a highly respected family of old Austria. I remembered that a bearer of that name had been an intimate friend of Schubert, and that one of the old Emperor's physicians-in-ordinary had belonged to the same family. Dr B was visibly dumbfounded when I stated our wish that he should take Czentovic on. It proved that he had no idea that he had stood his ground against a champion, let alone the most famous one in the world at the moment. For some reason this news seemed to make a special impression on him, for he inquired once and again whether I was sure that his opponent was truly a recognised holder of international honours. I soon perceived that this circumstance made my mission easier, but sensing his refined feelings, I considered it discreet to withhold the fact that McConnor would be a pecuniary loser in case of an eventual defeat. After considerable hesitation Dr B at last consented to a match, but with the proviso that my fellow-players be warned against putting extravagant hope in his expertness.

"Because," he added with a clouded smile, "I really don't know whether I have the ability to play the game according to all the rules. I assure you that it was not by any means false modesty that made me say that I hadn't touched a chess-man since my college days, say more than twenty years. And even then I had no particular gifts as a player." This was said so simply that I had not the slightest doubt of its truth. And yet I could not but express wonderment at his accurate memory of the details of positions in games by many different masters; he must, at least, have been greatly occupied with chess theory. Dr B smiled once more in that dreamy way of his.

"Greatly occupied! Heaven knows, it's true enough that I have occupied myself with chess greatly. But that happened under quite special, I might say unique, circumstances. The story of it is rather complicated and it might go as a little chapter in the story of our agreeable epoch. Do you think you would have patience for half an hour? ... "

He waved towards the deck-chair next to his. I accepted the invitation gladly. There were no near neighbours. Dr B removed his reading spectacles, laid them to one side, and began.

"You were kind enough to say that, as a Viennese, you remembered the name of my family. I am pretty sure, however, that you could hardly have heard of the law office which my father and I conducted—and later I alone—for we had no cases that got into the papers and we avoided new clients on principle. In truth, we no longer had a regular law practice but confined ourselves exclusively to advising, and mainly to administering the fortunes of the great monasteries with which my father, once a Deputy of the Clerical Party, was closely connected. Besides—in this day and generation I am no longer obliged to keep silence about the Monarchy—we had been entrusted with the investment of the funds of certain members of the Imperial family. These connections with the Court and the Church—my uncle had been the Emperor's household physician, another was an abbot in Seitenstetten —dated back two generations; all we had to do was to maintain them, and the task allotted to us through this inherited confidence—a quiet, I might almost say a soundless, task—really called for little more than strict discretion and dependability, two qualities which my late father possessed in full measure; he succeeded, in fact, through his prudence in preserving considerable values for his clients through the years of inflation as well as the period of collapse. Then, when Hitler seized the helm in Germany and began to raid the properties of churches and cloisters, certain negotiations and transactions, initiated from the other side of the frontier with a view to saving at least the movable valuables from confiscation, went through our hands and we two knew more about sundry secret transactions between the Curia and the Imperial house than the public will ever learn. But the very inconspicuousness of our office—we hadn't even a sign on the door—as well as the care with which both of us almost ostentatiously kept out of Monarchist circles, offered the safest protection from officious investigations. In fact, no Austrian official had ever suspected that during all those years the secret couriers of the Imperial family delivered and fetched their most important mail in our unpretentious fourth-floor office.

It happened that the National Socialists began, long before they armed their forces against the world, to organize a

different but equally schooled and dangerous army in all neigh-
bouring countries—the legion of the unprivileged, the despised,
the injured. Their so-called 'cells' nested themselves in every
office, in every business; they had listening-posts and spies in
every spot, right up to the private chambers of Dollfuss and
Schuschnigg. They had their man, as alas, I learned only too
late, even in our insignificant office. True, he was nothing but a
wretched, ungifted clerk whom I had engaged, on the recom-
mendation of a priest, for no other purpose than to give the office
the appearance of a going concern; all that we really used him
for was innocent errands, answering the telephone, and filing
papers, that is to say papers of no real importance. He was not
allowed to open the mail. I typed important letters myself and
kept no copies. I took all essential documents to my home, and I
held private interviews nowhere but in the priory of the cloister
or in my uncle's consultation-room. These measures of cau-
tion prevented the listening-post from seeing anything that went
on; but some unlucky happening must have made the vain and
ambitious fellow aware that he was mistrusted and that interesting things were going on behind his back. It may have been that
in my absence one of the couriers made a careless reference to
'His Majesty' instead of the stipulated 'Baron Bern,' or that the
rascal opened letters surreptitiously. Whatever the reason, before
I had so much as suspected him, he managed to get a mandate
from Berlin or Munich to watch us. It was only much later, long
after my imprisonment began, that I remembered how his early
laziness at work had changed in the last few months to a sudden eagerness when he frequently offered, almost intrusively,
to post my letters. I cannot acquit myself of a certain amount
of imprudence, but after all, haven't the greatest diplomats and
generals of the world also been out-manoeuvred by Hitler's cunning? Just how precisely and lovingly the Gestapo had long been
directing its attention to me was manifested tangibly by the fact
that the SS people arrested me on the evening of the very day

of Schuschnigg's abdication, and a day before Hitler entered Vienna. Luckily I had been able to burn the most important documents upon hearing Schuschnigg's farewell address over the radio, and the other papers, along with the indispensable vouchers for the securities held abroad for the cloisters and two archdukes, I concealed in a basket of laundry which my faithful housekeeper took to my uncle. All of this almost literally in the last minute before the fellows broke my door down."

Dr B interrupted himself long enough to light a cigar. I noticed by the light of the match a nervous twitch at the right corner of his mouth that had struck me before and which, as far as I could observe, recurred every few minutes. It was merely a fleeting vibration, hardly stronger than a breath, but it imparted to the whole face a singular restlessness.

"I suppose you expect that I'm going to tell you about the concentration camp to which all who held faith with our old Austria were removed; about the degradations, martyrings and tortures that I suffered there. Nothing of the kind happened. I was in a different category. I was not put with those luckless ones on whom they released their accumulated resentment by corporal and spiritual degradation, but rather was assigned to that small group out of which the National Socialists hoped to squeeze money or important information. My obscurity in itself meant nothing to the Gestapo, of course. They must have guessed, though, that we were the dummies, the administrators and confidants, of their most embittered adversaries, and what they expected to extract from me was incriminating evidence, evidence against the monasteries to support charges of violation by those who had selflessly taken up the cudgels for the Monarchy. They suspected, and not without good reason, that a substantial portion of the funds that we handled was still secreted and inaccessible to their lust for loot—hence their choice of me on the very first day in order to force the desired information by their trusted methods. That is why persons of my sort, to whom they looked for money or significant evidence, were not dumped into a concentration camp but were sorted out for special handling. You will recall that our Chancellor, and also Baron Rothschild, from whose family they hoped to extort millions, were not planted behind barbed wire in a prison camp but, ostensibly privileged, were lodged in individual rooms in a hotel, the Metropole, which happened to be the Gestapo headquarters. The same distinction was bestowed on my insignificant self.

A room to oneself in a hotel—sounds pretty decent, doesn't it? But you may believe me that they had not in mind a more decent but a more crafty technique when, instead of stuffing us 'prominent' ones in blocks of twenty into icy barracks, they housed us in tolerably heated hotel rooms, each by himself. For the pressure by which they planned to extract the needed testimony was to be exerted more subtly than through common beating or physical torture: by the most conceivably complete isolation. They did nothing to us; they merely deposited us in the midst of nothing, knowing well that of all things the most potent pressure on the soul of man is nothingness. By placing us singly, each in an utter vacuum, in a chamber that was hermetically closed to the world without, it was calculated that the pressure created from inside, rather than cold and the scourge, would eventually cause our lips to spring apart.

The first sight of the room allotted to me was not at all repellent. There was a door, a table, a bed, a chair, a wash-basin, a barred window. The door, however, remained closed night and day; the table remained bare of book, newspaper, pencil, paper; the window gave on to a brick wall; my ego and my physical self were contained in a structure of nothingness. They had taken every object from me: my watch, that I might not know the hour; my pencil, that I might not make a note; my pocket-knife, that I might not sever a vein; even the slight narcotic of a cigarette was forbidden me. Except for the warder, who was not permitted to address me or to answer a question, I saw no human face, I heard no human voice. From dawn to dusk there was no sustenance for eye or ear or any sense; I was alone with myself, with my body and four or five inanimate things, rescuelessly alone with table, bed, window, and basin. One lived like a diver in his bell in the black ocean of this silence— like a diver, too, who is dimly aware that the cable to safety has already snapped and that he never will be raised from the soundless depths. There was nothing to do, nothing to hear, nothing to see; about me, everywhere and without interruption, there was nothingness, emptiness without space or time. I walked to and fro, and with me went my thoughts, to and fro, to and fro, again and again. But even thoughts, insubstantial as they seem, require an anchorage if they are not to revolve and circle around themselves; they too weigh down under nothingness. One waited for something from morn to eve and nothing happened. Nothing happened. One waited, waited, waited; one thought, one thought, one thought until one's temples smarted. Nothing happened. One remained alone. Alone. Alone.

That lasted for a fortnight, during which I lived outside of time, outside the world. If war had broken out then I would never have discovered it, for my world comprised only table, door, bed, basin, chair, window and wall, every line of whose scalloped pattern embedded itself as with a steel graver in the innermost folds of my brain every time it met my eye. Then, at last, the hearings began. Suddenly I received a summons; I hardly knew whether it was day or night. I was called and led through a few corridors, I knew not whither; then I waited and knew not where it was, and found myself standing at a table behind which some uniformed men were seated. Piles of papers on the table, documents of whose contents I was in ignorance; and then came the questions, the real ones and the false, the simple and the cunning, the catch questions and the dummy questions; and whilst I answered, strange and evil fingers toyed with papers whose contents I could not surmise, and strange evil fingers wrote a record and I could not know what they wrote. But the most fearsome thing for me at those hearings was that I could never guess or figure out what the Gestapo actually knew about the goings-on in my office and what they sought to worm out of me. I have already told you that at the last minute I gave my housekeeper the really incriminating documents to take to my uncle. Had he received them? Had he not received them? How far had I been betrayed by that clerk? Which letters had they intercepted and what might they not already have screwed out of some clumsy priest at one of the cloisters which we represented?

And they heaped question upon question. What securities had I bought for this cloister, with which banks had I corresponded, do I know Mr So-and-so or do I not, had I corresponded with Switzerland and with God-knows-where? And not being able to divine what they had already dug up, every answer was fraught with danger. Were I to admit something that they didn't know I might be unnecessarily exposing somebody to the axe. If I denied too much I harmed myself.

The worst was not the examination. The worst was the return from the examination to my void, to the same room with the same table, the same bed, the same basin, the same wallpaper. No sooner was I by myself than I tried to recapitulate, to think of what I should have said and what I should say next time so as to divert any suspicion that a careless remark of mine might have aroused. I pondered, I combed through, I probed, I appraised every single word of testimony before the examining officers. I went over their every question and every answer that I made. I sought to sift out the part that went into the protocol, knowing well that it was all incalculable and unascertainable.

But these thoughts, once given rein in empty space, whirred in my head unceasingly, always starting afresh in ever-changing combinations and insinuating themselves into my sleep.

After every hearing by the Gestapo my own thoughts took over no less inexorably the torturing questions, searchings and torments, and perhaps even more horribly, for the hearings at least ended after an hour, but this repetition, thanks to the spiteful torture of solitude, never ended. And always the table, chest, bed, wallpaper, window; no diversion, not a book or magazine, not a new face, no pencil with which to jot down an item, not a match to toy with—nothing, nothing, nothing. It was only at this point that I apprehended how devilishly intelligently, with what murderous psychology, this hotel room system was conceived. In a concentration camp one would, perhaps, have had to wheel stones until one's hands bled and one's feet froze in one's boots; one would have been packed in stench and cold with a couple of dozen others. But one would have seen faces, would have had space, a tree, a star, something, anything, to stare at, while here everything stood before one unchangeably the same, always the same, maddeningly the same. There was nothing here to switch me off from my thoughts, from my delusive notions, from my diseased recapitulating. That was just what they intended: they wanted me to gag and gag on my thoughts until they choked me and I had no choice but to spit them out at last, to admit—admit everything that they were after, finally to yield up the evidence and the people.

I gradually became aware of how my nerves were slacking under the grisly pressure of the void and, conscious of the danger, I tensed myself to bursting point in an effort to find or create any sort of diversion. I tried to recite or reconstruct everything I had ever memorised in order to occupy myself—the folk songs and nursery rhymes of childhood, the Homer of my high-school days, clauses from the Civil Code. Then I did problems in arithmetic, adding or dividing, but my memory was powerless without some integrating force. I was unable to concentrate on anything. One thought flickered and darted about: how much do they know? What is it that they don't know? What did I say yesterday—what ought I to say next time?

This simply indescribable state lasted four months. Well, four months; easy to write, just about a dozen letters! Easy to say, too: four months, a couple of syllables. The lips can articulate the sound in a quarter of a second: four months. But nobody can describe or measure or demonstrate, not to another or to himself, how long a period endures in the spaceless and timeless, nor can one explain to another how it eats into and destroys one, this nothing and nothing and nothing that is all about, everlastingly this table and bed and basin and wallpaper, and always that silence, always the same warder who shoves the food in without looking at one, always those same thoughts that revolve around one in the nothingness, until one becomes insane.

Small signs made me unnervingly conscious that my brain was not working right. Early in the game my mind had been quite clear at the examinations; I had testified quietly and deliberately; my twofold thinking—what should I say and what not?—had still functioned. Now I could no more than articulate haltingly the simplest sentences, for while I spoke my eyes were fixed in a hypnotic stare on the pen that sped across the paper as if I wished to race after my own words. I felt myself losing my grip, I felt that the moment was coming closer and closer when, to rescue myself, I would tell all I knew and perhaps more; when, to elude the strangling grip of that nothingness, I would betray twelve persons and their secrets without deriving any advantage myself but the respite of a single breath.

One evening I really reached that limit: the warder had just served my meal at such a moment of desperation when I suddenly shrieked after him: 'Take me to the Board! I'll tell everything! I want to confess! I'll tell them where the papers are and where the money is! I'll tell them everything! Everything!' Fortunately he was far enough away not to hear me. Or perhaps he didn't want to hear me.

An event occurred in this extremest need, something unforeseeable, that offered rescue, rescue if only for a period. It was late in July, a dark, ominous, rainy day: I recall these details quite definitely because the rain was rattling against the windows of the corridor through which I was being led to the cross-examination. I had to wait in the ante-room of the audience chamber. Always one had to wait before the session; the business of letting one wait was a trick of the game. They would first rip one's nerves by the call, the abrupt summons from the cell in the middle of the night, and then, by the time one was keyed to the ordeal with will and reason tensed to resistance, they caused one to wait, meaningless meaningful waiting, an hour, two hours, three hours before the trial, to weary the body and humble the spirit. And they caused me to wait particularly long on this Thursday, the 27th of July; twice the hour struck while I attended, standing, in the ante-room; there is a special reason, too, for my remembering the date so exactly.

A calendar hung in this room—it goes without saying that they never permitted me to sit down; my legs bored into my body for two hours—and I find it impossible to convey to you how my hunger for something printed, something written, made me stare at these figures, these few words, '27 July,' against the wall; I wolfed them into my brain. Then I waited some more and waited and looked to see when the door would open at last, meanwhile reflecting on what my inquisitors might ask me this time, knowing well that they would ask me something quite different from that for which I was schooling myself. Yet in the face of all that, the torment of the waiting and standing was nevertheless a blessing, a delight, because this room was, after all, a different one from my own, somewhat larger and with two windows instead of one, and without the bed and without the basin and without that crack in the window-sill that I had looked at a million times. The door was painted differently, a different chair stood against the wall, and to the left stood a filing cabinet with documents as well as a clothes-stand on which three or four wet military coats hung—my torturers' coats. So that I had something new, something different to look at, at last something different for my starved eyes, and they clawed greedily at every detail.

I took in every fold of those garments; I observed, for example, a drop suspended from one of the wet collars and, ludicrous as it may sound to you, I waited with an inane excitement to see whether the drop would eventually detach itself and roll down or whether it would resist gravity and stay put; truly, this drop held me breathless for minutes, as if my life had been at stake. It rolled down after all, and then I counted the buttons on the coats again, eight on one, eight on another, ten on the third, and again I compared the rank marks; all of these absurd and unimportant trifles toyed with, teased, and pinched my ravenous eyes with an avidity which I forgo trying to describe. And suddenly I saw something that paralysed my gaze. I had discovered a slight bulge in the sidepocket of one of the coats. I moved closer to it and thought that I recognised, by the rectangular shape of the protrusion, what this swollen pocket concealed: a book! My knees trembled: a BOOK!

I hadn't had a book in my hand for four months, so that the mere idea of a book in which words appear in orderly arrangement, of sentences, pages, leaves, a book in which one could follow and stow in one's brain new, unknown, diverting thoughts, was at once intoxicating and stupefying. Hypnotised, my eyes rested on the little swelling which the book inside the pocket formed; they glowered at the spot as if to burn a hole in the coat. The moment came when I could no longer control my greed; involuntarily I edged nearer. The mere thought that my hands might at least feel the book through the cloth made the nerves of my fingers tingle to the nails. Almost without knowing what I did, I found myself getting closer to it.

Happily the warder ignored my singular behaviour; indeed, it may have seemed to him quite natural that a man wanted to lean against a wall after standing erect for two hours. And then I was quite close to the coat, my hands purposely clasped behind me so as to be able to touch the coat unnoticed. I felt the stuff and the contact confirmed that here was something square, something flexible, and that it crackled softly—a book, a book! And then a thought went through me like a shot: steal the book! If you're smart you can hide the book in your cell and read, read, read—read again at last. The thought, barely conceived, operated like a virulent poison; at once there was a singing in my ears, my heart hammered, my hands froze and resisted my bidding. But after that first numbness I pressed myself softly and insinuatingly against the coat; I coaxed— always fixing the warder with my eye—the book up out of the pocket, higher and higher, with my artfully concealed hands. Then: a tug, a gentle, careful pull, and in no time the little book was in my hand. Not until now was I frightened at my deed. Retreat was no longer possible. What to do with it? I shoved the book under my trousers at the back just far enough for the belt to hold it, then gradually to the hip so that while walking I could keep it in place by holding my hands on the trouser-seams, military fashion. I had to try it out, so I moved a step from the clothes-stand, two steps, three steps. It worked. It was possible to keep the book in place while walking if I kept pressing firmly against my belt.

Then came the hearing. It demanded greater attention than ever on my part, for while answering I concentrated my entire effort on securing the book inconspicuously rather than on my testimony. Luckily this session proved to be a short one and I got the book safely to my room, though it slipped into my trousers most alarmingly while in the corridor on my way back and I had to feign a violent fit of coughing as an excuse for bending over to get it under my belt again. But what a moment, that, as I carried it back into my inferno, alone at last yet no longer alone!

You will suppose, of course, that my first act was to seize the book, examine it and read it. Not at all! I wanted, first of all, to savour the joy of possessing a book; the artificially prolonged and nerve-inflaming desire to daydream about the kind of book I would wish this stolen one to be: above all, very small type, narrowly spaced, with many, many letters, many, many thin leaves so that it might take long to read. And then I wished to myself that it might be one that would demand mental exertion, nothing smooth or light; rather something from which I could learn and memorise, preferably—oh, what an audacious dream!—Goethe or Homer. At last I could no longer check my greed and my curiosity. Stretched on the bed so as to arouse no suspicion in case the warder might open the door without warning, tremblingly I drew the volume from under my belt.

The first glance produced not merely disappointment but a sort of bitter vexation, for this booty, whose acquiring was surrounded with such monstrous danger and such glowing hope, proved to be nothing more than a chess anthology, a collection of one hundred and fifty championship games. Had I not been barred, locked in, I would, in my spontaneous rage, have thrown the thing through an open window; for what was to be done—what could be done—with nonsense of the kind? Like most of the other boys at school, I had now and then tried my hand at chess to kill time. But of what use was this theoretical stuff to me? You can't play chess alone, and certainly not without chess-men and a board. Annoyed, I thumbed the pages, thinking to discover reading matter of some sort, an introduction, a manual; but, besides the bare rectangular reproductions of the various master games with their symbols—**a2-a3**, **Sf1-g3**, etc—to me then unintelligible, I found nothing. All of it appeared to me as a kind of algebra the key to which was hidden. Only gradually I puzzled out that the letters **a**, **b**, **c** stood for the vertical rows, the figures **1** to **8** for the rows across, and indicated the current position of each figure; thus these purely graphic expressions did, nevertheless, make a modicum of sense.

Who knows, I thought, if I were able to devise a chess-board in my cell I could follow these games through; and it seemed like a sign from heaven that the weave of my bedspread disclosed a coarse chequer-work. With proper manipulation it yielded a field of sixty-four squares. I tore out the first page and concealed the book under my mattress. Then, from bits of bread that I sacrificed, I began to mould king, queen, and the other figures (with ludicrous results, of course), and after no end of effort I was finally able to undertake on the bedspread the reproduction of the positions pictured in the chess book. But my absurd doughy figures, half of which I had covered with dust to differentiate them from 'white' ones, proved utterly inadequate when I tried to pursue the printed game. I was all confusion in those first days; I would have to start a game afresh five times, ten times, twenty times. But who on earth had so much unused and useless time as I, slave of emptiness, and who commanded so much immeasurable greed and patience!

It took me six days to play the game to the end without an error, and in a week after that I no longer required the chessmen to fathom the relative positions, and in just one more week I was able to dispense with the bedspread; the printed symbols, **a1**, **a2**, **c7**, **c8**, at first abstractions to me, automatically transformed themselves into visual positions. The transposition had been accomplished perfectly. I had projected the chess-board and its figures within myself and, thanks to the bare rules, observed the immediate set-up just as a practised musician hears all instruments singly and in combination upon merely glancing at a printed score.

It cost me no effort, after another fortnight, to play every game in the book from memory or, in chess language, blind; and only then did I begin to understand the limitless benefaction which my impertinent theft constituted. For I had acquired an occupation—a senseless, a purposeless one if you wish—yet one that negated the nothingness that enveloped me; the one hundred and fifty championship games equipped me with a weapon against the strangling monotony of space and time.

From then on, to conserve the charm of this new interest without interruption, I divided my day precisely: two games in the morning, two in the afternoon, a quick recapitulation in the evening. That served to fill my day which previously had been as shapeless as jelly; I had something to do that did not tire me, for a wonderful feature of chess is that through confining mental energy to a strictly bounded field the brain does not flag even under the most strained concentration; rather it makes more acute its agility and energy. In the course of time the repetition of the master games, which had at first been mechanical, awakened an artistic, a pleasurable comprehension in me. I learned to understand the refinements, the tricks and strategies in attack and defence; I grasped the technique of thinking ahead, planning combinations and riposting, and soon recognised the personal note of each champion in his individual method as infallibly as one spots a particular poet on hearing only a few lines. That which began as a mere time-killing occupation became a joy, and the personalities of such great chess strategists as Alekhin, Lasker, Boguljobov and Tartakover entered into my solitude as beloved comrades.

My silent cell was constantly and variously peopled, and the very regularity of my exercises restored my already impaired intellectual capacity; my brain seemed refreshed and, because of constant disciplined thinking, even keenly whetted. My ability to think more clearly and concisely manifested itself, above all, at the hearings; unconsciously I had perfected myself at the chess-board in defending myself against false threats and masked dodges; from this time on I gave them no openings at the sessions and I even harboured the thought that the Gestapo men began, after a while, to regard me with a certain respect. Possibly they asked themselves, seeing so many others collapse, from what secret sources I alone found strength for such unshakeable resistance.

This period of happiness in which I played through the one hundred and fifty games in that book systematically, day by day, continued for about two and a half to three months. Then I arrived unexpectedly at a dead point. Suddenly I found myself once more facing nothingness. For by the time that I had played through each one of these games innumerable times, the charm of novelty and surprise was lost, the exciting and stimulating power was exhausted. What purpose did it serve to repeat again and again games whose every move I had long since memorised? No sooner did I make an opening move than the whole thing unravelled of itself; there was no surprise, no tension, no problem. At this point I would have needed another book with more games to keep me busy, to engage the mental effort that had become indispensable to divert me. This being totally impossible, my madness could take but one course: instead of the old games I had to devise new ones myself. I had to try to play the game with myself or, rather, against myself.

I have no idea to what extent you have given thought to the intellectual status of this game of games. But one doesn't have to reflect deeply to see that if pure chance can determine a game of calculation, it is an absurdity in logic to play against oneself. The fundamental attraction of chess lies, after all, in the fact that its strategy develops in different ways in two different brains, that in this mental battle Black, ignorant of White's immediate manoeuvres, seeks constantly to guess and cross them, while White, for his part, strives to penetrate

Black's secret purposes and to outstrip and parry them. If one person tries to be both Black and White you have the preposterous situation that one and the same brain at once knows something and yet does not know it; that, functioning as White's partner, it can instantly obey a command to forget what, a moment earlier as Black's partner, it desired and plotted. Such cerebral duality really implies a complete cleavage of the conscious, a lighting up or dimming of the brain function at pleasure as with a switch; in short, to want to play against oneself at chess is about as paradoxical as to want to jump over one's own shadow.

Well, in short, in my desperation I tried this impossibility, this absurdity, for months. There was no choice but this nonsense if I was not to become quite insane or slowly to disintegrate mentally. The fearful state that I was in compelled me at least to attempt this split between Black ego and White ego so as not to be crushed by the horrible nothingness that bore in on me."

Dr B relaxed in his deck-chair and closed his eyes for a minute. It seemed as if he were exerting his will to suppress a disturbing recollection. Once again the left corner of his mouth twitched in that strange and evidently uncontrollable manner. Then he settled himself a little more erectly.

"Well, then, I hope I've made it all pretty intelligible up to this point. I'm sorry, but I doubt greatly that the rest of it can be pictured quite as clearly. This new occupation, you see, called for so unconditional a harnessing of the brain as to make any simultaneous self-control impossible. I have already intimated my opinion that a chess contest with oneself spells nonsense, but there is a minimal possibility for even such an absurdity if a real chess-board is present, because the board, being tangible, affords a sense of distance, a material extra-territoriality.

Before a real chess-board with real chess-men you can stop to think things over, and you can place yourself physically first on this side of the table, then on the other, to fix in your eyes how the scene looks to Black and how it looks to White. Obliged as I was to conduct these contests against myself—or with myself, as you please—on an imaginary field, so I was obliged to keep fixedly in mind the current set-up on the sixty-four squares and, besides, to make advance calculations as to the possible further moves open to each player, which meant—I know how mad this must sound to you—imagining doubly, triply, no, imagining sextuply, duodecimally for each one of my egos, always four or five moves in advance.

Please don't think that I expect you to follow through the intricacies of this madness. In these plays in the abstract space of fantasy I had to figure out the next four or five moves in my capacity of White, likewise as Black, thus considering every possible future combination with two brains, so to speak, White's brain and Black's brain. But even this auto-cleaving of personality was not the most dangerous aspect of my abstruse experiment; rather it was that with the need to play independently I lost my foothold and fell into a bottomless pit. The mere replaying of championship games, which I had been indulging in during the preceding weeks, had been, after all, no more than a feat of repetition, a straight recapitulation of given material and, as such, no greater strain than to memorise poetry or learn sections of the Civil Code by heart; it was a delimited, disciplined function and thus an excellent mental exercise. My two morning games, my two in the afternoon, represented a definite task that I was able to perform coolly; it was a substitute for normal occupation and, moreover, if I erred in the progress of a game or forgot the next move, I always had recourse to the book. It was only because the replaying of others' games left myself out of the picture that this activity served to soothe and heal my shattered nerves; it was all the same to me whether

Black or White was victor, for was it not Alekhin or Boguljobov who sought the palm, while my own person, my reason, my soul derived satisfaction as observer, as fancier of the niceties of those jousts as they worked out. From the moment at which I tried to play against myself I began, unconsciously, to challenge myself. Each of my egos, my Black ego and my White ego, had to contest against the other and become the centre, each on its own, of an ambition, an impatience to win, to conquer; after each move that I made as Ego Black I was in a fever of curiosity as to what Ego White would do. Each of my egos felt triumphant when the other made a bad move and likewise suffered chagrin at similar clumsiness of its own.

All that sounds senseless, and in fact such a self-produced schizophrenia, such a split consciousness with its fund of dangerous excitement, would be unthinkable in a person under normal conditions. Don't forget, though, that I had been violently torn from all normality, innocently charged and behind bars, for months martyrised by the refined employment of solitude—a man seeking an object against which to vent his long-accumulated rage. And as I had nothing else than this insane match with myself, that rage, that lust for revenge, channelled itself fanatically into the game. Something in me wanted to justify itself, but there was only this other self with which I could wrestle; so while the game was on, an almost maniac excitement grew in me. In the beginning my deliberations were still quiet and composed, I would pause between one game and the next so as to recover from the effort; but little by little my frayed nerves forbade all respite. No sooner had Ego White made a move than Ego Black feverishly plunged a piece forward; scarcely had a game ended but I challenged myself to another, for each time, of course, one of my chess-egos was beaten by the other and demanded satisfaction.

I shall never be able to tell, even approximately, how many games I played against myself during those months in my cell as a result of this crazy insatiability; a thousand perhaps, perhaps more. It was an obsession against which I could not arm myself; from dawn to dusk I thought of nothing but knights and pawns, rooks and kings, and **a**, **b** and **c**, and 'check-mate!' and 'castle'; my entire being and every sense embraced the chequered board. The joy of play became a lust for play; the lust for play became a compulsion to play, a frenetic rage, a mania which saturated not only my waking hours but eventually my sleep, too. I could think only in terms of chess, only in chess moves, chess problems; sometimes I would wake with a damp brow and become aware that a game had unconsciously continued in my sleep, and if I dreamed of persons it was exclusively in the moves of the bishop, the rook, in the advance and retreat of the knight's move.

Even when I was brought before the examining board I was no longer able to keep my thoughts within the bounds of my responsibilities; I'm inclined to think that I must have expressed myself confusedly at the last sessions, for my judges would glance at one another strangely. Actually I was merely waiting, while they questioned and deliberated, in my cursed eagerness to be led back to my cell so that I could resume my mad round, to start a fresh game, and another and another. Every interruption disturbed me; even the quarter-hour in which the warder cleaned up the room, the two minutes in which he served my meals, tortured my feverish impatience; sometimes the midday meal stood untouched on the tray at evening because the game made me forgetful of food. The only physical sensation that I experienced was a terrible thirst; the fever of this constant thinking and playing must already have manifested itself then; I emptied the bottle in two gulps and begged the warder for more, and nevertheless felt my tongue dry in my mouth in the next minute.

Finally my excitement during the games rose—by that time I did nothing else from morning till night—to such a height that

I was no longer able to sit still for a minute; uninterruptedly, while cogitating on a move, I would walk to and fro, quicker and quicker, to and fro, to and fro, and the nearer the approach to the decisive moment of the game the hotter my steps; the lust to win, to victory, to victory over myself swelled to a sort of rage; I trembled with impatience, for the one chess-ego in me was always too slow for the other. One would whip the other forward and, absurd as this may seem to you, I would call angrily, 'Quicker, quicker!' or 'Go on, go on!' when the one self in me failed to respond to the other's thrust quickly enough. It goes without saying that I am now fully aware that this state of mine was nothing less than a pathological form of overwrought mind for which I can find no other name than one not yet known to medical annals: chess poisoning.

The time came when this monomania, this obsession, attacked my body as well as my brain. I lost weight, my sleep was restless and disturbed, upon waking I had to make great efforts to compel my leaden eyelids to open; sometimes I was so weak that when I clutched a glass I could scarcely raise it to my lips, my hands trembled so; but no sooner did the game begin than a mad power seized me: I rushed up and down, up and down with fists clenched, and I would sometimes hear my own voice as through a reddish fog, shouting hoarsely and angrily at myself, 'check!' or 'check-mate!'

How this horrible, indescribable condition reached its crisis is something that I am unable to report. All that I know is that I woke one morning and the waking was different from usual. My body was no longer a burden, so to speak; I rested softly and easily. A tight, agreeable fatigue, such as I had not known for months, lay on my eyelids; the feeling was so warm and benign that I couldn't bring myself to open my eyes. For minutes I lay awake and continued to enjoy this heavy soddenness, this wallowing in agreeable stupefaction. All at once I seemed to hear voices behind me, living human voices, low whispering voices that spoke words; and you can't possibly imagine my delight, for months had elapsed, perhaps a year, since I had heard other words than the hard, sharp, evil ones from my judges. 'You're dreaming,' I said to myself. 'You're dreaming! Don't, in any circumstances, open your eyes. Let the dream last or you'll again see the cursed cell about you, the chair and wash-stand and the table and the wallpaper with the eternal pattern. You're dreaming—keep on dreaming!'

But curiosity had the upper hand. Slowly and carefully I opened my eyes. A miracle! It was a different room in which I found myself, a room wider and more ample than my hotel cell. An unbarred window admitted light freely and permitted a view of trees, green trees swaying in the wind, instead of my bald brick partition; the walls shone white and smooth, above me a high white ceiling. I lay in a new and unaccustomed bed and—surely, it was no dream—human voices whispered behind me.

In my surprise I must have made an abrupt, involuntary movement, for at once I heard an approaching step. A woman came softly, a woman with a white headdress, a nurse, a Sister. A delighted shudder ran through me: I had seen no woman for a year. I stared at the lovely apparition, and it must have been a glance of wild ecstasy, for she admonished me, 'Quiet, don't move.' I hung only on her voice for here was a person who talked! Was there still somebody on earth who did not interrogate me, torture me? And to top it all—ungraspable wonder!—a soft, warm, almost tender woman's voice. I stared hungrily at her mouth, for the year of inferno had made it seem to me impossible that one person might speak kindly to another. She smiled at me—yes, she smiled; then there still were people who could smile benevolently—put a warning finger to her lips, and went off without a sound. But I could not obey her order; was not yet sated with the miracle. I tried to wrench myself into a sitting posture so as to follow with my eyes this wonder of a human being who was kind. But when I reached out to support my weight on the edge of the bed something failed me. In place of my right hand, fingers, and wrist I became aware of something foreign—a thick, large, white lump, obviously a bandage. At first I gaped uncomprehendingly at this bulky object, then slowly I began to grasp where I was and to reflect on what could have happened to me. They must have injured me, or I had done some damage to my hand myself. The place was a hospital.

The physician, an amiable elderly man, turned up at noon. He knew my family and made so genial an allusion to my uncle, the Imperial household doctor, as to create the impression that he was well disposed towards me. In the course of conversation he asked all sorts of questions, one of which, in particular, astonished me: Was I a mathematician or a chemist? I answered in the negative.

'Strange,' he murmured. 'In your fever you cried out such unusual formulas, **c3**, **c4**. We could make nothing of it.'

I asked him what had happened to me. He smiled oddly.

'Nothing too serious. An acute irritation of the nerves,' and added in a low voice, after looking carefully around, 'and quite understandable, of course. Let's see, it was 13th March wasn't it!'

I nodded.

'No wonder, with that system,' he admitted. 'You're not the first. But don't worry.' The manner of his soothing speech and sympathetic smile convinced me that I was in a safe haven.

A couple of days later the doctor told me quite of his own accord what had taken place. The warder had heard shrieks from my cell and thought, at first, that I was disputing with somebody who had broken in. But no sooner had he shown himself at the door than I made for him, shouted wildly something that sounded like 'Aren't you ever going to move, you rascal, you coward?' lunged at his throat, and finally attacked him so ferociously that he had to call for help. Then when they were dragging me, in my mad rage, for medical examination, I had suddenly broken loose and thrust myself against the window in the corridor, thereby lacerating my hand; see this deep scar. I had been in a sort of brain fever during the first few days in the hospital, but now he found my perceptive faculties quite in order. 'To be sure,' he said *sotto voce*, 'it's just as well that I don't report that higher up or they may still come and fetch you back there. Depend on me, I'll do my best.'

Whatever it was that this benevolent doctor told my torturers about me is beyond my knowledge. In any case, he achieved what he sought to achieve: my release. It may be that he declared me not responsible for my actions, or it may be that my importance to the Gestapo had diminished, for Hitler had since occupied Bohemia, thus liquidating the case of Austria. I had merely to sign an undertaking to leave the country within a fortnight, and this period was so filled with the multitude of formalities that now surround a journey—military certificate, police, tax and health certificates, passport, visas—as to leave me no time to brood over the past. Apparently one's brain is controlled by secret, regulatory powers which automatically switch off whatever may annoy or endanger the mind, for every time I wanted to ponder on my imprisonment the light in my brain seemed to go off; only after many weeks, indeed only now, on this ship, have I plucked up enough courage to contemplate all that I lived through."

"After all this you will understand my unbecoming and perhaps strange conduct to your friends. It was only by chance that I was strolling through the smoking-room and saw them sitting at the chess-board; my feet seemed rooted where I stood from astonishment and fright. For I had totally forgotten that one can play chess with a real board and real figures, forgotten that two physically separate persons sit opposite each other at this game. Truly, it took me a few minutes before I remembered that what those men were playing was what I had been playing, against myself during the months of my helplessness. The cipher-code which served me in my worthy exercises was but a substitute, a symbol for these solid figures; my astonishment that this pushing about of pieces on the board was the same as the wild imaginings in my mind must have been like that of an astronomer who, after complicated calculations on paper as to the existence of a new planet, eventually really sees it in the sky as a clear, white, substantial body. I stared at the board as if magnetised and saw there my set-up, knight, rook, king, queen, and pawns, as genuine figures carved out of wood. In order to get the hang of the game I had voluntarily to transmute it from my abstract realm of numbers and letters into the movable figures. Gradually I was overcome with curiosity to observe a real contest between two players. Then followed that regrettable and impolite interference of mine with your game. But that mistaken move of your friend's was like a stab at my heart. It was pure instinct that made me hold him back, a quite impulsive grasp like that with which one involuntarily seizes a child leaning over a banister. It was not until afterwards that I became conscious of the impropriety of my intrusiveness."

I hastened to assure Dr B that we were all happy about the incident to which we owed his acquaintance and that, after what he had confided in me, I would be doubly interested in the opportunity to see him at tomorrow's improvised tournament.

"Really, you mustn't expect too much. It will be nothing but a test for me—a test whether I—whether I'm at all capable of dealing with chess in a normal way, in a game with a real board with substantial chess-men and a living opponent—for now I doubt more than ever that those hundreds, they may have been thousands, of games that I played were actual games according to the rules and not merely a sort of dream-chess, fever-chess, a delirium in which, as always in dreams, one skips intermediate steps. Surely you do not seriously believe that I would measure myself against a champion, that I expect to give tit for tat to the greatest one in the world. What interests and fascinates me is nothing but the posthumous curiosity to discover whether what went on in my cell was chess or madness, whether I was then at the dangerous brink or already beyond it—that's all, nothing else."

At this moment the gong summoning passengers to dinner was heard. The conversation must have lasted almost two hours, for Dr B had told me his story in much greater detail than that in which I assemble it. I thanked him warmly and took my leave. I had hardly covered the length of the deck when he was alongside me, visibly nervous, saying with something of a stutter:

"One thing more. Will you please tell your friends beforehand, so that it should not later seem discourteous, that I will play only one game ... The idea is merely to close an old account—a final settlement, not a new beginning ... I can't afford to sink back a second time into that passionate play-fever that I recall with nothing but horror. And besides—besides, the doctor warned me, expressly warned me. Everyone who has ever succumbed to a mania remains for ever in jeopardy, and a sufferer from chess poisoning—even if discharged as cured—had better keep away from a chess-board. You understand, then— only this one experimental game for myself and no more."

We assembled in the smoking-room the next day promptly at the appointed hour, three o'clock. Our circle had increased by yet two more lovers of the royal game, two ship's officers who had obtained special leave from duty to watch the tourney. Czentovic, too, not as on the preceding days, was on time. After the usual choice of colours there began the memorable game of this *homo obscurissimus* against the celebrated master.

I regret that it was played for thoroughly incompetent observers like us, and that its course is as completely lost to the annals of the art of chess as are Beethoven's improvisations to music. True, we tried to piece it together from our collective memory on the following afternoons, but in vain; very likely, in the passion of the moment, we had allowed our interest to centre on the players rather than on the game. For the intellectual contrast between the contestants became physically plastic according to their manner as the play proceeded. Czentovic, the creature of routine, remained the entire time as immobile as a block, his eyes unalterably fixed on the board; thinking seemed to cost him almost physical effort that called for extreme concentration on the part of every organ. Dr B, on the other hand, was completely slack and unconstrained. Like the true dilettante, in the best sense of the word, to whom only the play in play—the *diletto*—gives joy, he relaxed fully, explained moves to us in easy conversation during the early intervals, lighted a cigarette carelessly, and glanced at the board for a minute only when it came his turn to play. Each time it seemed as if he had expected just the move that his antagonist made.

The perfunctory moves came off quite rapidly. It was not until the seventh or eighth that something like a definite plan seemed to develop. Czentovic prolonged his periods of reflection; by that we sensed that the actual battle for the lead was setting in. But, to be quite frank, the gradual development of the situation represented to us lay observers, as usually in tournament games, something of a disappointment. The more the pieces wove themselves into a singular design the more impenetrable became the real lie-of-the-land. We could not discern what one or the other rival purposed or which of the two had the advantage. We noticed merely that certain pieces insinuated themselves forward like levers to undermine the enemy front, but since every move of these superior players was part of a combination that comprised a plan for several moves ahead, we were unable to detect the strategy of their back-and-forth.

An oppressive fatigue took possession of us, largely because of Czentovic's interminable cogitation between moves, which eventually produced visible irritation in our friend too. I observed uneasily how, the longer the game stretched out, he became increasingly restless, moving about in his chair, nervously lighting a succession of cigarettes, occasionally seizing a pencil to make a note. He would order mineral water and gulp it down, glass after glass; it was plain that his mind was working a hundred times faster than Czentovic's. Every time the latter, after endless reflection, decided to push a piece forward with his heavy hand, our friend would smile like one who encounters something long expected and make an immediate riposte. In his nimble mind he must have calculated every possibility that lay open to his opponent; the longer Czentovic took to make a decision the more his impatience grew, and during the waiting his lips narrowed into an angry and almost inimical line. Czentovic, however, did not allow himself to be hurried. He deliberated, stiff and silent, and increased the length of the pauses the more the field became denuded of figures. By the forty-second move, after one and a half hours, we sat limply by, almost indifferent to what was going on in the arena. One of the ship's officers had already departed, another was reading a book and would look up only when a piece had been moved. Then suddenly, at a move of Czentovic's, the unexpected happened. As soon as Dr B perceived that Czentovic took hold of the bishop to move it, he crouched like a cat about to spring. His whole body trembled and Czentovic had no sooner executed his intention than he pushed his queen forward and said loudly and triumphantly, "There! That's done with," fell back in his chair, his arms crossed over his breast, and looked challengingly at Czentovic. As he spoke his pupils gleamed with a hot light.

127

Impulsively we bent over the board to figure out the significance of the move so ostentatiously announced. At first blush no direct threat was observable. Our friend's statement, then, had reference to some development that we short-thoughted amateurs could not anticipate. Czentovic was the only one among us who had not stirred at the provocative call; he remained as still as if the insulting 'done with' had glanced off him unheard. Nothing happened. Everybody held his breath and at once the ticking of the clock that stood on the table to measure the moves became audible. Three minutes passed, seven minutes, eight minutes—Czentovic was motionless, but I thought I noticed an inner tension that became manifest in the greater distension of his thick nostrils.

This silent waiting seemed to be as unbearable to our friend as to us. He shoved his chair back, rose abruptly and began to traverse the smoking-room, first slowly, then quicker and quicker. Those present looked at him wonderingly, but none with greater uneasiness than I, for I perceived that in spite of his vehemence this pacing never deviated from a uniform span; it was as if, in this confined space, he would each time come plump against an invisible cupboard that obliged him to reverse his steps. Shuddering, I recognised that it was an unconscious reproduction of the pacing in his erstwhile cell; during those months of incarceration it must have been exactly thus that he rushed to and fro, like a caged animal; his hands must have been clenched and his shoulders hunched exactly like this; it must have been like this that he pelted forward and back a thousand times there, the red lights of madness in his paralysed though feverish stare. Yet his mental control seemed still fully intact, for from time to time he turned impatiently towards the table to see if Czentovic had made up his mind. But time stretched to nine, then ten minutes.

What occurred then, at last, was something that none could have predicted. Czentovic slowly raised his heavy hand, which, until then, had rested inert on the table. Tautly we all watched for the upshot. Czentovic, however, moved no piece, but instead, with the back of his hand pushed, with one slow determined sweep, all the figures from the board. It took us a moment to comprehend: he gave up the game. He had capitulated in order that we might not witness his being mated. The impossible had come to pass: the champion of the world, victor at innumerable tournaments, had struck his colours before an unknown man, who hadn't touched a chess-board for twenty or twenty-five years. Our friend, the anonymous, the *ignotus*, had overcome the greatest chess master on earth in open battle.

Automatically, in the excitement, one after another rose to his feet; each was animated by the feeling that he must give vent to the joyous shock by saying or doing something. Only one remained stolidly at rest: Czentovic. After a measured interval he lifted his head and directed a stony look at our friend.

"Another game?" he asked.

"Naturally," answered Dr B with an enthusiasm that was disturbing to me, and he seated himself, even before I could remind him of his own stipulation to play only once, and began to set up the figures in feverish haste. He pushed them about in such a frenzy that a pawn twice slid from his trembling fingers to the floor; the pained discomfort that his unnatural excitement had already produced in me grew to something like fear. For this previously calm and quiet person had become visibly exalted; the twitching of his mouth was more frequent and in every limb he shook as with fever.

"Don't," I said softly to him. "No more now; you've had enough for today. It's too much of a strain for you."

"Strain! Ha!" and he laughed loudly and spitefully. "I could have played seventeen games during that slow ride. The only strain is for me to keep awake—Well, aren't you ever going to begin?"

These last words had been addressed in an impetuous, almost rude tone to Czentovic. The latter glanced at him quietly and

evenly, but there was something of a clenched fist in that ada-
mantine, stubborn glance. On the instant a new element had
entered: a dangerous tension, a passionate hate. No longer
were they two players in a sporting way; they were two enemies
sworn to destroy each other. Czentovic hesitated long before
making the first move, and I had a definite sensation that he
was delaying on purpose. No question but that this seasoned
tactician had long since discovered that just such dilatoriness
wearied and irritated his antagonist. He used no less than four
minutes for the normal, the simplest of openings, moving the
king's pawn two spaces. Instantly our friend advanced his king's
pawn, but again Czentovic was responsible for an eternal,
intolerable pause; it was like waiting with beating heart for the
thunder-clap after a streak of fiery lightning, and waiting—
with no thunder forthcoming. Czentovic never stirred. He
meditated quietly, slowly, and as I felt, increasingly, maliciously
slowly—which gave me plenty of time to observe Dr B. He
had just about consumed his third glass of water; it came to my
mind that he had spoken of his feverish thirst in his cell. Every
symptom of abnormal excitement was plainly present: I saw
his forehead grow moist and the scar on his hand become red-
der and more sharply outlined. Still, however, he held himself
in rein. It was not until the fourth move, when Czentovic again
pondered exasperatingly, that he forgot himself and exploded
with, "Aren't you ever going to move?"

Czentovic looked up coldly. "As I remember it, we agreed on a
ten-minute limit. It is a principle with me not to make it less."

Dr B bit his lips. I noticed under the table the growing restlessness with which he lifted and lowered the sole of his shoe, and
I could not control the nervousness that overcame me because
of the oppressive prescience of some insane thing that was
boiling in him. As a matter of fact, there was a second encounter
at the eighth move. Dr B, whose self-control diminished with
the increasing periods of waiting, could no longer conceal his

tension; he was restless in his seat and unconsciously began to drum on the table with his fingers. Again Czentovic raised his peasant head.

"May I ask you not to drum. It disturbs me. I can't play with that going on."

"Ha, ha," answered Dr B with a short laugh, "one can see that."

Czentovic flushed. "What do you mean by that?" he asked, sharply and evilly.

Dr B gave another curt and spiteful laugh. "Nothing except that it's plain that you're nervous."

Czentovic lowered his head and said nothing. Seven minutes elapsed before he made his move, and that was the funereal tempo at which the game dragged on. Czentovic became correspondingly stonier; in the end he utilised the maximum time before determining on a move, and from interval to interval the conduct of our friend became stranger and stranger. It appeared as if he no longer had any interest in the game but was occupied with something quite different. He abandoned his excited pacing and remained seated motionlessly. Staring into the void with a vacant and almost insane look, he uninterruptedly muttered unintelligible words; either he was absorbed in endless combinations or—and this was my inner suspicion—he was working out quite other games, for each time that Czentovic got to the point of making a move he had to be recalled from his absent state. Then it took a minute or two to orient himself. My conviction grew that he had really forgotten all about Czentovic and the rest of us in this cold aspect of his insanity which might at any instant discharge itself violently. Surely enough, at the nineteenth move the crisis came. No sooner had Czentovic executed his play than Dr B, giving no more than a cursory look at the board, suddenly pushed his bishop three spaces forward and shouted so loudly that we all started "Check! check, the king!"

Every eye was on the board in anticipation of an extraordinary move. Then, after a minute, there was an unexpected development. Very slowly Czentovic tilted his head and looked —which he had never done before—from one face to another. Something seemed to afford him a rich enjoyment, for little by little his lips gave expression to a satisfied and scornful smile. Only after he had savoured to the full the triumph which was still unintelligible to us did he address us, saying with mock deference:

"Sorry—but I see no check. Perhaps one of you gentlemen can see my king in check?"

We looked at the board and then uneasily over at Dr B. Czentovic's king was fully covered against the bishop by a pawn—a child could see that—thus the king could not possibly be in check. We turned one to the other. Might not our friend in his agitation have pushed a piece over the line, a square too far one way or the other? His attention arrested by our silence, Dr B now stared at the board and began, stutteringly:

"But the king ought to be on **f7**—that's wrong, all wrong— Your move was wrong! All the pieces are misplaced—the pawn should be on **g5** and not on **g4**. Why, that's quite a different game—that's—"

He halted abruptly. I had seized his arm roughly, or rather I had pinched it so hard that even in his feverish bewilderment he could not but feel my grip. He turned and looked at me like a somnambulist.

"What—what do you want?"

I only said "Remember!" at the same time lightly drawing my finger over the scar on his hand. Automatically he followed my gesture, his eyes fixed glassily on the blood-red streak. Suddenly he began to tremble and his body shook.

"For God's sake," he whispered with pale lips. "Have I said or done something silly? Is it possible that I'm again? ... "

"No," I said, in a low voice, "but you have to stop the game at once. It's high time. Remember what the doctor said."

With a single movement Dr B was on his feet. "I have to apologise for my stupid mistake," he said in his old, polite voice, inclining himself to Czentovic. "What I said was plain nonsense, of course. It goes without saying that the game is yours." Then to us: "My apologies to you gentlemen, also. But I warned you beforehand not to expect too much from me. Forgive the disgrace—it is the last time that I yield to the temptation of chess."

He bowed and left in the same modest and mysterious manner in which he had first appeared before us. I alone knew why this man would never again touch a chess-board, while the others, a bit confused, stood around with that vague feeling of having narrowly escaped something uncomfortable and dangerous. "Damned fool," McConnor grumbled in his disappointment.

Last of all, Czentovic rose from his chair, half glancing at the unfinished game.

"Too bad," he said generously. "The attack wasn't at all badly conceived. The man certainly has lots of talent for an amateur."